ALSO BY ANNIE BARROWS

The Magic Half

c.2

Magic in the Mix

ANNIE BARROWS

BLOOMSBURY
NEW YORK   LONDON   NEW DELHI   SYDNEY

First published in the United States of America in September 2014
by Bloomsbury Children's Books
www.bloomsbury.com

Bloomsbury is a registered trademark of Bloomsbury Publishing Plc

For information about permission to reproduce
selections from this book, write to
Permissions, Bloomsbury Children's Books,
1385 Broadway, New York, New York 10018
Bloomsbury books may be purchased for business or promotional use.
For information on bulk purchases please contact Macmillan Corporate and
Premium Sales Department at specialmarkets@macmillan.com

Library of Congress Cataloging-in-Publication Data
Barrows, Annie.
Magic in the mix / by Annie Barrows.
pages   cm
Sequel to: The magic half.
Summary: Life seems to be back to normal for "newly twinned"
sisters Miri and Molly until their magical house sends them
on a new time-traveling adventure to the Civil War, where they
must risk everything to save two unusual soldiers and come
to terms with the emotional truth about Molly's past.
ISBN 978-1-61963-482-4 (hardcover) • ISBN 978-1-61963-483-1 (e-book)
[1. Twins—Fiction. 2. Sisters—Fiction. 3. Time travel—Fiction.
4. Magic—Fiction. 5. United States—History—Civil War,
1861–1865—Fiction.] I. Title.
PZ7.B27576Mb 2014   [Fic]—dc23   2014005032

Typeset by Westchester Book Composition
Printed and bound in the U.S.A. by Thomson-Shore Inc., Dexter, Michigan
2 4 6 8 10 9 7 5 3 1

For Jeffrey again

❦ CHAPTER ❧

1

"I think I hear them," said Molly.

Miri listened. "No," she said after a moment. "If it were them, they'd be yelling."

The two girls waited patiently on the front steps. Sort of patiently. Not so patiently. On the hard, cold steps.

"They'd better be grateful," muttered Molly. "My tush is going to sleep."

"Mine's frozen," Miri grumbled.

All at once, two boys exploded into the front yard. Skinny and shouting, they sprinted up the sloping lawn toward the house, trying to hit each other as they ran.

Miri and Molly rose to their feet. Each of them

held a piece of paper. On Miri's, in big black letters, was the word PROGRESS. On Molly's, in the same big black letters, was the word REPORTS.

"And he's down!" screeched Robbie, dragging his brother, Ray, backward by the strap of his backpack until he collapsed. "He's down in the dumps! He's a loser! He's—" Robbie glanced up and froze.

Ray took the opportunity to hook his foot around Robbie's ankle, but before he could flip his brother over, he, too, caught sight of his sisters. "Oh, man," he said under his breath.

Miri and Molly flipped the papers over. MOM, said one. RAGING, said the other.

Ray and Robbie nodded slowly. Thanks, they mouthed, and turned to slink toward the tangle of blackberry coils and apple trees that grew wild on one side of the yard, the traditional hiding place for Gill children waiting out a parental storm.

The front door opened, and a small blond head poked out. "Ooooh, they're *home*! Mommy's really mad at you!"

"Shut *up*!" moaned Ray. But it was too late. They all heard the clatter of their mother's shoes hurrying down the hall.

Miri winced in sympathy. "We tried."

Robbie nodded, his face glum.

And here came Mom's voice, shooting out the front door ahead of her. "How on *earth* is it *possible* that you boys got Fs—*Fs!*—in history? Just come right into this house, the pair of you"—now she burst into view, hands waving—"and I'll make one thing perfectly clear! There will be no, I repeat, *no* sports, including cross-country, until you earn at *least* a B in history! Am I making myself understood?" She stood on the porch, her hands on her hips, her eyes flashing.

Ray and Robbie knew better than to argue. "Right, Mom," they mumbled. "Sorry, Mom."

But she was too mad to stop. Their father said she was like a music box; once she was wound up, she had to keep going until she ran down. "Of course I immediately made a call to Mr. Emory"—Ray and Robbie gulped—"and I learned, to my *horror*, that the pair of you not only flunked, *flunked*, your last test, but you cut class as well!"

"Only once!" protested Ray.

"Ooh, bad move," whispered Miri to Molly.

She was right. "*Once!*" squawked their mother. "*Once is one time too many, Raymond Gill!* Once! Once!"

"I don't know why he says things like that," Molly murmured to Miri.

"You'd think he'd learn," said Miri, shaking her head. "Check out Robbie."

Molly nodded appreciatively. "He's good."

"Sort of ashamed and pathetic at the same time," Miri said with admiration.

Their mother whirled around. "What are you two muttering about?"

Uh-oh. Trouble was contagious. Miri tried to look innocent.

"Miri and Molly were telling!" squealed Nora from the front door. "They had signs!"

Mom frowned. "What?"

"They had signs!" Nora repeated triumphantly. "They were telling Ray and Robbie things."

Miri took a breath, preparing her denial, but Molly laughed. "You goof," Molly said to Nora. "We were doing homework. See?" She picked up her conveniently located math book and waved it at Nora. "We were multiplying percentages."

Her mother's frown disappeared, and Miri marveled. Quick thinking was Molly's specialty. When trouble reared its ugly head, Molly decided what to do and did it, pronto. Miri, on the other hand, was usually thinking about something else and taken completely by surprise. Miri was good at imagining possibilities; Molly was good at dealing with realities. As Molly showed Nora a page of math problems, Miri thought, Molly's a genius at evading trouble. And Miri knew why, too. Molly had had a lot of practice.

"Good!" said Mom approvingly. "Excellent! Multiplying percentages is very important!" She slapped her hands together, full of energy. "Everyone inside! Time for homework!"

"I'm only five," Nora gloated to her older brothers and sisters. "Five-year-olds don't have any homework."

Mom patted her cheek. "They do now."

. . .

An hour later, when their father came in, they were still at the kitchen table, all six of them, doing their homework.

"These are my kids," he said, waving his hand casually at the kitchen table. "Kids, this is Ollie." He gestured to a wiry man beside him. "Ollie's going to be helping me with the porch stairs." Their father continued toward the back door.

Ollie didn't. Ollie came to a halt in the middle of the kitchen and frowned. Miri watched him counting. Comparing heights. Comparing faces. And then counting once again. His frown got squintier and squintier.

Why not get it over with, thought Miri. "Three sets of twins," she called helpfully.

He shook his head. "No way."

"Way," said Ray.

"Way," echoed Robbie.

Nell and Nora nodded. Way.

Their father's head reappeared in the doorframe. "Um, Ollie? The porch is back here."

Ollie swung around. "Three? Three sets of twins?"

Dad grinned. "That's right."

Miri and Molly looked up, waiting. Ray and Robbie did the same. Even Nell and Nora paused in the midst of their massive pasting project. What was it going to be this time? Ollie didn't look like the kind of person who would say, "Oh my! What a lovely surprise that must have been!" Mostly, it was little old ladies who said that.

He also didn't look like he was going to say "Better you than me, man," which was what a waiter had said one time, probably because Nell had dropped two enchiladas on the floor at the exact same moment that Nora had thrown up.

Once, a man had kissed their mother's hand. "Madame," he had said, "you are magnificent." She had liked that.

Ollie continued to inspect them, chewing on his mustache thoughtfully. "Huh," he said, waggling a finger from Ray and Robbie to Nell and Nora. "Those ones look alike." The finger waggled toward Miri and Molly. "And those ones don't."

"That's right," said their father. "Identical, fraternal, identical. Statistically rare. Actually, statistically anomalous, with an incidence of . . ."

Ollie obviously didn't care about statistics. His eyes roved over the six children as their father spoke, and finally he made his pronouncement: "There's always something been funny about this house. Guess you're it now." And with that, he turned and slouched toward the back porch.

"That was random," said Ray, rolling his eyes.

Nell looked with satisfaction at the mountain of sticky paper in front of her. "I like homework."

"I like paste," said Nora.

As their brothers and sisters bent over their work, Miri and Molly exchanged quick sideways glances tinged with alarm. Something funny about the house? How did Ollie know about the house? And what did he know? Was it possible that he knew the truth?

Impossible. Only Miri and Molly knew that.

Only they knew that there had not always been three sets of twins in the Gill family. Only they knew that once, not too long ago, there had been just two pairs of twins: Ray and Robbie, Nell and Nora. And Miri in the middle, the single child between the pairs, alone and lonely, excluded from the world of her brothers, too old for the world of her sisters. All that, everything she had called family, had changed in one day, a bizarre day when time had collapsed, and Miri had found herself standing in her own bedroom in the year 1935. There, she'd met a girl her own age, a girl named Molly Gardner. It had been magic, of course, a kind of time-magic, but Miri soon learned that the magic hadn't been given to her simply for entertainment. Magic didn't waste itself like that. It wanted something from her, as magic always did. It wanted Miri to trick time, to take Molly Gardner away from the danger that she faced in 1935, from her scary cousin Horst and her nasty aunt Flo. And after that, the magic wanted Miri to bring Molly home.

Together, Miri and Molly had puzzled out the rules of magic, piece by piece, until they'd opened a door in time, a door just big enough to slip through. Then they'd changed history, giving Molly a new past and Miri a new twin. In the process, they'd turned the Gills from an unusual family, with two sets of twins, to a positively extraordinary family, with three.

And only Miri and Molly knew that it had happened. Everyone else thought that Molly had always been Miri's twin.

Of course, there were clues, a few loose ends that might have been noticeable, if anyone had been in a noticing frame of mind. As Ollie had pointed out, they weren't identical twins, and the others were. Miri's eyes were green; Molly's, gray. Though they both had brown hair, Molly's was straight and streaked with gold, while Miri's drove her bonkers by curling wildly in some places and lying flat in others. As a girl who'd grown up in the thirties, Molly had a dress-wearing habit that was hard to break. Miri usually wore jeans. But the differences weren't huge, and they made themselves look alike by getting the same round glasses and wearing their hair in braids. They felt like twins, they looked like sisters, and no one thought a thing of it.

Sometimes the secret threatened to burst free—not because they wanted to tell it, but because it was so enormous. Miri snatched at the words as they fell out of her mouth—"back when I was alone" or "before Molly got here"—and hastily changed them into something that sounded reasonable. More often, it was Molly who slipped into the wrong century: "She's a real humdinger," she'd say absentmindedly, watching Beyoncé. Or she'd sing advertising jingles for products that had disappeared by 1940. Once, she had said something about "the forty-eight states," and Miri had kicked her, hard, in the ankle. But as the months passed, Molly's 1930s childhood became less and less real; her time with Miri—the lifetime of shared memories that had been created the moment she'd passed into the Gill family—became stronger and stronger. Even so, for both girls, the easiest time of day was the end, when they stretched out in their bunk beds and talked about what had happened to them.

"Everyone in the whole world wishes for magic," Miri had said one night. Her voice had drifted through the darkness, filled with wonder. "And we got it. How lucky is that?"

"Pretty lucky," said Molly. "Pretty incredibly lucky. Especially for me."

"Pooh," said Miri. "Especially for me. I got a sister. I got a *twin*. And I got to go back in time." She let out a long breath, remembering it—the shimmering moment when she and Molly had realized that magic was real and it had happened to them. "We'd be crazy to think that it would ever happen again. To us, I mean."

"It could," said Molly.

"It probably won't," said Miri. She rolled over and looked out the high round window of their room. The moon fit perfectly inside it. Could you wish upon the moon? She decided you could. Let magic happen to us one more time, she begged. Please. And if you take requests, I'd like to go back and hang out with the Indians. The American ones, please. Thank you. "Do you think I'm being greedy even to want it?"

"No," Molly said at once. "Remember what Grandma said—magic is just a way of setting things right. Remember?"

"I remember," said Miri. Molly's 1935 grandmother, May, had known all the secrets of magic. It was Grandma May who had told them they were meant to be sisters.

"Well, see, that's it," said Molly. "If magic happens to us again, it will be because we're supposed to set something right."

Miri brightened. "So it wouldn't be greedy, would it? Because we'd be doing good." Maybe she could bring the smallpox vaccine to the Indians. "We wouldn't be just playing around, having a good time. We'd have a task. We'd be in the line of duty."

Molly snickered. "Gee, it sounds really un-fun when you put it like that."

"It could be fun, too," said Miri, picturing herself gliding silently through a moon-silvered forest with a bow slung over her shoulder. "But even if it isn't," she added, "we'll have to do whatever the magic wants us to do. I mean, I think we owe it something for letting you come here. Don't you?"

"Yeah." Miri heard Molly flop over and pummel her pillow into shape. "Sometimes . . ." She paused.

"What?" Miri prodded.

"I sometimes wonder if . . ." Another uneasy pause.

"What?" urged Miri, curious. Molly was usually the opposite of hesitant.

"Sometimes I wonder if I'm supposed to be here. If I'm going to be allowed to stay. I mean," Molly said hastily, "I *want* to be here, but why can I remember both worlds? Why does the magic let me remember being a kid in the thirties *and* being a kid with you and Mom and Dad?"

"Oh. Yeah. I remember both, too," Miri said. She gazed at the moon. "I remember walking into kindergarten on the first day holding your hand, and I remember walking into kindergarten the first day with just Mom. I guess it means that both things actually did happen."

Molly sat up abruptly. "But don't you think that's weird? If the magic really meant it, we shouldn't remember both lives. Nobody has two pasts. We should only remember this life, the one together."

Now Miri sat up, too. There was something worrisome in Molly's tone. As if she doubted the new life would last. "Well," Miri said slowly, "I guess it's a little weird, but I think that the magic lets us remember both because we're the ones who made it happen. We know too much to forget it."

"That sounds like we're secret agents or something," Molly said doubtfully.

"We *are* like secret agents." Miri pounced on the idea. "We have double identities. We're the only people in the world with two pasts."

"I guess so," Molly agreed. "But that's what's bizarre. How can they both be true? It's like two pieces of train track coming together: first we were separate, and then we joined, but we're the only ones who can see both tracks. For everyone else, there's just one track."

Miri thought about that for a moment. "I picture it more like a cake."

"A cake? What's a cake?"

"Time. It's like the layers of a cake. In my mind, all of time, all the people who ever lived, and everything that ever happened in all of history is still going on, but in separate layers, stacked one on top of the other, like a cake. Right at this moment, it's also a million years ago and yesterday and 1935 and every other time, too."

"Crowded cake," said Molly.

"No, because see, all the layers are separate, so everyone thinks that theirs is the only layer."

"Okay, time's a cake," said Molly. "But I still don't get why you and I can see more than one layer."

"The layers of time are separate from one another," Miri continued, "just like frosting separates the layers of a cake. But I think there are certain places where the frosting between the layers is very, very thin. Those are places where one time can mix into another. I think our house is one of those places."

Silence from the bottom bunk. Then Molly said slowly, "Grandma said something like that. Remember? She said, 'Time means nothing in this house.'"

"Yeah, and she knew more about magic than anyone," Miri said.

"Huh." Molly flopped back down. "Layers of time. That's pretty good. First our times were separate, but now they're mixed together."

"Yeah," said Miri. "That's it. That's why we can see both times."

"In a way, we've had two lives," said Molly thoughtfully.

Miri hesitated. "Which life is better?"

She had never asked that before; it had seemed

too private. But there was no hesitation in Molly's voice as she replied, "Well, gee, let's see: In this life, I've got you. And a mom and a dad and two cute little sisters and two dorky but funny brothers. In my first life, I had no mom; a missing dad; Aunt Flo, who hated me; and a cousin who was trying to beat me up all the time. And, oh yeah, it was during the Depression, so I was really poor. It's a tough call."

Miri dangled her head over the side of the bed. "It's better for me, too," she said happily. "It's better for all of us."

Molly's voice came again in the darkness. "I have a family now. I didn't really know what that meant before. To have people be *glad* to see me every day—I didn't know about that." There was a silence, and then she said, "Sometimes I'm scared it's all going to disappear. You know, like maybe I'm going to wake up in 1935."

"No. You came through. This is your time now," Miri said. "And you're supposed to be here. Grandma May said so. She said we were setting things right."

"Yeah," said Molly. "I guess so. But she also said I might see her again someday. Remember?"

"Yes." Miri would never forget that scene. Molly's

grandmother, her eyes glinting like jewels, her worn hand cradling Molly's cheek as she said, "Do you think a little thing like time can separate us?"

Now, at the table with her brothers and sisters, her homework forgotten, Miri glanced around the old kitchen before coming back to Molly. They shared a long look, and each knew what the other was thinking: There *is* something funny about this house. Us.

THE NEXT DAY, Shenandoah Middle School was exactly the way it usually was: okay. Miri and Molly were in the sixth grade now, moving from class to class—though never the same class at the same time (they suspected a grown-up plot, but they couldn't prove it). As experienced middle schoolers, Robbie and Ray had given them many valuable tips the night before school began: "Don't go to the bathroom alone," "Don't slam ketchup packets inside your books," "Don't let anyone stuff you in your locker," "Don't fart during science," "Don't talk to eighth graders, especially Daggie."

None of these tips had proved to be very useful, except maybe "Don't fart during science." Going to the bathroom alone was impossible. The place was always packed with girls putting on lip gloss.

As her final class of the day, Health and Nutrition, inched toward its conclusion, Miri slid ever farther downward in her stiff wooden seat until only her eyes remained above the sea-level of her desktop. I'm sinking, she thought, into a shark-infested sea. She folded a piece of paper into a fin and bobbed it lazily across the sea. Blub, glub, "Glub," she mumbled aloud.

"Yes! Miri!" Miss Roos whirled around. "How many?"

Miri shot upright. "Eight!" she cried, hoping her answer had something to do with the question.

"Wow!" enthused Miss Roos. "Eight servings of fruit or vegetables a day! That's great!" She smiled around the classroom. "Miri's got the healthy eating habit, doesn't she?"

Everyone glared at Miri. Whoops, she thought, smiling apologetically at the girl sitting next to her. I've got to stop saying the first thing that pops into my head. She reflected that she probably did eat eight helpings of fruits and vegetables a day. But she wasn't supposed to say so; it looked like sucking up. Middle school was complicated. A lot like a shark-infested sea, she thought, and slid sleepily downward again.

At the day's end, Molly was waiting for Miri outside the classroom. "Scale of one to ten?" she called when she saw Miri.

"Six," yawned Miri.

"Same here." Together, they gathered their books from their lockers, ran to catch the bus, and joggled along the highway to the town of Paxton. There, they got off bus number one, spent five minutes staring wistfully at the candy in Mike's Snak-n-Go, got on bus number two, and set off down the long, zigzagging country road that led home. The nice thing about living so far out in the valley was how pretty it was—lots of trees, turning now to gold and red, and tiny creeks dodging in and out of rolling hills. The not-so-nice thing was how long it took to get there.

But as soon as she rounded the hedge that bordered the driveway and caught a glimpse of her house, Miri decided, as she always did, that it was worth a bus ride of almost any length. Sitting on a slight hill above a sloping circle of lawn in the shade of an enormous elm tree, the house was big, old, shabby, and beautiful, with its lacy wooden trim edging the roof, its panes of colored glass bordering the door, and its curtain of vines shading the deep front porch. Miri loved everything about it, from the odd ten-sided room she shared with Molly to the wreaths carved into the mantelpiece in the living room. She loved the dust-smelling attic, she loved the hammock on the porch, she even loved the decrepit faucets that came off in your hand if you turned the water on too hard. It was rich with old-ness, her house.

"Home again," murmured Molly, with a long, contented sigh. "Home."

Miri nodded. "Home—" She broke off, startled by the whack of a hammer resounding through the yard. Then came a long, wooden ripping noise. The two girls exchanged looks of alarm—earthquake? Tornado? Giants? Following the trail of sound, they ran up the lawn and veered around the side of the house to the backyard—

Where they skidded to a halt, astonished by the wreckage. The back porch, which had that morning stretched across the rear of the house, lay in bits on the ground. Dark boards had been hurled into a mangled heap on the grass, while a tidy stack of fresh pink wood sat primly to one side. The destroyed porch had been almost a room, with shelves, cupboards, and windows on three sides. Now the windows, still in their frames, were propped against the side of the house for reuse. A pile of shelves and a stack of cupboard doors had been dumped helter-skelter into the weedy grass.

"Look at the door," Molly gasped.

The back door, which had opened from the kitchen onto the porch only that morning, now opened onto nothing but air. The old white door, flapping six feet above the ground, looked silly now, like something in a cartoon.

In the center of the emptiness where the porch had been stood Dad and Ollie, chucking rocks and hunks of wood on the mountain of remains. "Girls!" called Dad enthusiastically. "Isn't this outstanding?"

"You said you were just fixing the stairs," Miri said, frowning. "You didn't say you were going to tear the whole porch down."

He straightened, rubbing his back. "I didn't know I was going to tear it down, either. But once we got going, Ollie saw a lot of dry rot. And wet rot, too, huh, Ollie?"

"Lots of rot," confirmed Ollie vigorously. He hurled a rock toward the pile. "Big-time rot."

"It had to come down before it fell down," their father said.

"But what about—history?" asked Molly. "What about heritage?"

"Heritage?" Her father blinked at her. "Well, think about it this way: I'm keeping our heritage from rotting. I'm saving it from itself."

"Rot's rot!" called Ollie with gusto. "You gotta dig it out. You gotta get it gone." He gazed at the newly exposed wall of the house and smacked his lips. Miri could tell he was dying to tear it apart and find more rot.

"Oh, hey!" said her father suddenly. "You want history? I found some old pictures and clippings when we were taking down the shelves. They're historical. I stuck them—" He looked around absently. "Where'd I stick them, Ollie?"

"On your new porch." Ollie pointed to the stack of fresh pink wood.

"Right! Go take a look. I thought your mom

might want them. She likes old stuff." He smiled, pleased with himself, and tossed a mushy-looking board on the junk heap.

Miri turned away. She wanted to argue, to save the house. She imagined herself standing bravely between the porch and Ollie, her palm up, the protector of the past. She looked up at the lonely, ridiculous door. "Sorry," she whispered.

"This stuff doesn't look right," said Molly, regarding the pink wood critically. "It's too new."

"Maybe the house will reject it," Miri said. She pictured a bone-shaking crash and a pile of pink splinters.

While Miri was having this pleasing vision, Molly was glancing through the little collection of papers. Suddenly, she giggled. "Check out this ad," she snickered, holding out a yellowed scrap of newspaper.

"'F. Gibbons, Undertaker and Furniture Manufactory,'" Miri read. A handsome dining room table was shown at the top of the ad, a roomy coffin at the bottom. She picked up a brownish photograph printed on cardboard. "Wow. Look at her." A scowling woman was packed tight into a black silk dress, her hair arranged in a mountain of oily curls. "I guess the smile-for-the-camera thing hadn't been invented yet."

"These guys are smiling." Molly tilted another photograph in Miri's direction, and Miri gazed at two young soldiers in dark uniforms. Like the woman, they were trying to look serious, but unlike her, they weren't succeeding. They'd pulled their caps down low over their eyes to look tough, but their mouths were bunched up, trying to hold back the laughter that was about to come bursting out. "Brothers," said Molly. "For sure."

"Maybe even twins," said Miri. She pulled the photo a little closer. "They look really alike." If she could see their eyes, she'd know for sure, but the caps were in the way.

Molly held up a picture of a tiny baby face engulfed in lace. "Boy or girl?"

Miri put down the laughing brothers. "I dunno," she said. "But whatever it is, it's mad." A piece of a board sailed past her head. "Dad!" she yelped, jumping back.

"Sorry! Forgot to look!" he called apologetically. "Maybe you guys should go inside, huh? You're probably supposed to do some homework anyway, right?"

They gave him injured looks. "Anyone would think you didn't want us here," called Molly.

"I don't," said Dad. "Go away." He bent to pick up a rock.

"You'll miss us when we're grown up," said Miri, and with one last, apologetic look at the dangling door, they swept away.

. . .

The two girls extended snack time to the farthest boundaries of the possible—apples and peanut butter with slow and refined chewing, chocolate milk with slow and unrefined slurping, an extended and unsuccessful search for cookies—but finally there was nothing left to do but sit down and face the bitter truth of math.

Robbie and Ray called to say they had missed the bus. Then they called to say that they had missed the next bus. Then they called to ask Mom to pick them up. Then they called to say that they didn't need her to pick them up, because the bus was coming. Then they called to ask if there was milk in the refrigerator.

"Milk?" asked Mom in confusion. "Why are you calling about milk? Come home and do your home-work!"

Miri and Molly exchanged tiny smiles and virtuously factored polynomials.

Time passed.

The phone rang.

"Why do you keep calling me about milk?" wailed Mom. "Yes! We have milk! We always have milk! Come home!"

A few minutes later, Ray and Robbie shuffled into the kitchen. As usual, their jeans sagged, their sweatshirts were scrawled with ink, and their hair stuck out in stiff, dirty sprigs from under their hats. Not as usual, they were walking very slowly, almost gently. Weirder still, they weren't yelling. They weren't squabbling. They weren't snorting or burping or grunting. They weren't making any noise at all. Miri watched in amazement as they glided in ghostly silence toward the table. What was the matter with them? Were they sick?

"There you are!" cried Mom in relief. "Now, I want you to sit right—"

"Shhh," murmured Robbie.

"It's sleeping," whispered Ray.

Mom froze. "Excuse me?"

Robbie slid toward the table without replying, and Miri saw that he had the dirtiest T-shirt in the world cupped in his hands. His eyes were shining with pride. "We got you guys something," he whispered.

"Us?" Molly was whispering, too.

He nodded. "A present. Because of yesterday." He tilted his head ever so slightly in the direction of their mother. "You know." Ray hung over Robbie's shoulder as he carefully set the dirty T-shirt on the table and opened it. There, rolled into a ball, was a very small, very white, very fluffy kitten.

"Ooooh," sighed Miri. "A *kitty*." Wonderstruck, she looked up at her brothers. "A baby kitty."

"Look!" Molly breathed. "Look at its baby paws."

As though it had heard, the kitten gave an arching, rigid stretch, and a tiny white paw quivered in the air. Miri couldn't help stretching out a finger to touch it. Round green eyes flew open and regarded her with astonishment. This was followed by a sneeze. Exhausted by this whirlwind of activity, the kitten sank back into sleep.

Mom peered around her sons. "You got them a *kitten*?" she gasped. "A *kitten*?"

"Yuh-huh," Ray said, beaming. "Pretty cute, huh?"

Miri held her breath. Please, please, please, she begged Mom silently. Please let us keep it. I'll be good for the rest of my life. I'll be good and kind and hardworking—

Then she saw her mother's face and knew that she didn't need to be good for the rest of her life. Mom bent over the kitten, enchanted. "Look at that little lovey," she murmured. With a single finger she stroked the fluff at the kitten's neck, cooing and clucking softly. Suddenly, there was a sniff, and Miri smiled as she saw her mother squeeze Ray's shoulder. "You boys," Mom choked, "you boys are sweethearts."

Behind Mom's head, Robbie gave his brother a thumbs-up. Score! he mouthed as Ray patted his mother's hand and tried to look sensitive.

"It's a girl," explained Robbie, glancing between Miri and Molly. "Like you guys." He pointed toward them, in case they hadn't noticed they were girls. "We thought that would be good." He gave the kitten a gentle pat. "That's good, huh?"

"Yeah," said Molly. "That's completely perfect."

"You guys are the best brothers in the world," said Miri, watching the soft fluff rise and fall.

Ray and Robbie smiled at each other smugly. They were the best brothers in the world. "We paid four dollars for her. Of our own money," said Robbie. They were generous, too.

"Where'd you get her?" murmured Mom, reaching out to stroke behind the kitten's tiny ear.

"Paxton. There was a guy outside the Snak-n-Go," explained Ray. "They were five dollars, but we talked him down to four."

"Oh, Lord, she probably has some horrible disease," sighed Mom, but Miri could tell she didn't need to worry. Her mother had begun to love the kitten, and once she started, she would never stop.

"The guy said to give her milk," said Robbie. He stared at the kitten and gave her another soft poke. "And jeez, me too. We spent all our money on the kitten, so we didn't get anything after school, and I'm gonna die of starvation in, like, four seconds." He moved toward the refrigerator.

Ray lunged after him. "I call the cereal if there's not enough for both of us."

"*Pfff,*" snorted Robbie, elbowing his brother in the ribs. Ray flicked his head. They were back to normal.

At the table, Molly and Miri hunched over their precious bundle, their brown hair falling together to make a little house for three.

. . .

It was hard to concentrate. Inside the dirty T-shirt, the kitten snoozed, first on Miri's lap and then on Molly's. Polynomials, factors, kitten, what should we name her, polynomials, what should we name her, look at her nose, it's so cute, factors, look at her ear, it twitched, what about Milly, sort of a combination of our names, that's cute, but would it be too confusing, maybe you're right, factors, what about—oh, look at her stretch!

"Mom better hurry up with that food," said Molly, glancing at the clock.

Kittens, it had turned out, needed other things besides milk. Including kitty litter. Miri and Molly had heroically volunteered to be peed and even pooped on while Mom took a quick trip to the store.

Ray looked up from his Spanish book. "You should call her Snowy. 'Cause see? She's white."

"Wow," said Molly. "That's really original."

"You like it?" he said, pleased.

Miri's eyes strayed to the cupboards they had unsuccessfully ransacked for cookies. "What about Cookie?"

"Cookie," said Molly experimentally. "That's kind of cute."

Miri stroked the warm bundle pressed against her stomach. "I think so, too. Cookie. Cookie," she cooed, "Cookie, Cookie-Wookie."

"How about Corn Chip?" said Robbie. He was hungry.

"No," said Molly. "Corn Chip sounds like we're about to eat her. Cookie."

"Cookie," agreed Miri, gently rubbing Cookie's chin. A small, rattling motor came to life in Cookie's throat.

"Or Burger," Robbie went on dreamily. "Or Pizza."

"No," said Miri. "Cookie."

The front door opened. "Guess what!" called their mother's voice. "I have, in one short hour, solved all of my children's problems." She clattered into the kitchen. "I solved yours." She smiled at Miri and Molly and dropped a pile of cat food, box, and litter onto the kitchen table. "And yours." She turned to Ray and Robbie.

"Our problem is we're hungry," said Robbie.

"No," said Mom. "Your problem is you're flunking history."

"It's called social studies now," said Ray.

"I call it history," said Mom. "And I just found a way for you to raise your grades." She looked energetically from son to son. "I ran into Mr. Emory at the grocery store"—Ray groaned—"Stop that. He seemed very nice. And he said that you can get extra credit by doing a Civil War reenactment this Saturday! Isn't that great?"

More groans.

"Now stop that! You don't even know what it is!"

"Yeah, we do," said Robbie. "It's this totally lame thing where a bunch of old guys get together and pretend that they're still fighting in a war that happened, like, two hundred years ago."

"A hundred and fifty years ago," corrected Mom. "A war that's extremely important in American history."

"They dress up." He snickered.

"You'll get extra credit," coaxed Mom.

"No," said Ray.

"You'll learn about the battles that happened around here." She smiled encouragingly.

"No," said Robbie.

"You'll get lots of exercise," she said.

"No," said Ray.

"You'll get guns," said a man's voice.

Ray and Robbie looked up. Ollie was standing in the doorway. "For real?" asked Ray.

"Yep. Course, they're not loaded, just with powder. Makes a pop, though." Ollie grinned as though this was good news. "You could get sabers, depending which company you're in. Probably you'll be Yankees. We never have enough Yankees."

"We don't mind being Yankees," said Ray. He looked at Robbie. "Do we?"

"Which ones are they?" asked Robbie.

Mom clapped her hand to her head. "No wonder you're flunking."

Ollie stared at Ray and Robbie, shocked. "The Yankees are the Northerners. The Union. The side that won," he said in a loud, distinct voice. "The Confederates are the Southerners. The ones that lost. The ones who lived here. Us." You idiots, his expression clearly added.

"Oh, yeah. Right," said Robbie. "We're in."

Ollie rolled his eyes and sloped off to the bathroom, muttering about kids today, and Miri shivered as one of the cold drafts that wafted through the old house curled along her neck. She picked up Cookie and huddled the kitten against her chest, where the downy fluff warmed her.

∿ CHAPTER ∿

3

DON'T SET THE HOUSE on fire. Miri and Molly nodded. But if you do set the house on fire, call us. Molly and Miri nodded. There's plenty to eat. Miri and Molly nodded. But don't just eat desserts; have some fruit. Molly and Miri nodded. Don't forget to feed Cookie. Miri and Molly nodded. But don't feed her before two. Molly and Miri nodded. If you have any problems, call us. Nod. Don't watch TV. Nod. You aren't allowed on the Internet when we aren't home. Nod, nod, nod.

Nod, nod, nod, nod, nod, nod, nod.

Now that it was Saturday, a warm, blue-skied October Saturday, Robbie and Ray were even less interested in their Civil War reenactment than they had been a few days before. They moped and shuffled and claimed to be getting sick and announced that life was unfair.

"It sure is," Dad agreed. "Get in the car."

And finally they did, looking very un-Civil-War-like in their jeans and sweatshirts, together with Mom and Dad and Nell and Nora, who were going to have a picnic while the fake armies battled.

"You'll be sorry if I get stabbed," whined Ray.

"If you get stabbed, Mommy will sew you up," Nell said confidently.

"Have *fun*!" trilled Molly and Miri from the front steps. "Learn lots of *history*!"

"Get out of here!" groaned Robbie, slumping into the backseat.

"I bet you'll look *darling* in your little costumes!" called Molly.

"Shut *up*," wailed Ray.

"Be sure to take pictures, Mom!" sang Miri. "So we can show them around school."

Their brothers' yelps of horror faded as the car crunched down the gravel driveway. Giggling, Molly and Miri turned toward the house.

Molly stretched luxuriously. "A whole day," she said.

"A whole day," Miri agreed. A whole day with the

house to themselves. In a family of eight, this was a rare and precious event. An opportunity. An occasion not to be squandered but to be spent judiciously in an activity that their parents would be happier if they didn't know about. Miri and Molly grinned at each other. They could do anything. They could do nothing. And whatever they did, no one would know!

They wandered through the living room aimlessly. "Let's bake something," suggested Miri. In her arms, Cookie purred, which, Miri decided, meant she thought Miri's idea was brilliant.

"Okay," said Molly. "Now that I don't have to do it all the time, I kind of miss baking."

"It's been almost eighty years," said Miri. "You remember how?"

They looked at each other gleefully—today, only today, they could talk about Molly's other life. Today they could say it out loud. Today they were free.

In the kitchen, they examined their supplies. "Let's bake cookies," suggested Molly. "You know, in honor of Cookie." Cookie raised her head. "Oh my gosh, look how smart she is! She knows her name already!"

Soon the kitchen counters were loaded with flour, butter, eggs, brown sugar, and chocolate chips. Even though there was nothing better in the world than chocolate chip cookie dough, they allowed themselves just one (extra-large) spoonful each. Cookie stepped delicately among the canisters, inspecting the ingredients and only once inserting her nose into the butter. Molly wiped the butter from the nose; Miri wiped the nose from the butter. They were a good team.

The day progressed, happy and easy. It was, Miri realized, exactly the kind of day she had dreamed of before Molly came. She had imagined how, if she had a twin, the two of them would sometimes talk and sometimes be quiet, how they'd have secret jokes that no one else knew, how they'd make plans, laugh, and just lie around together. And now she had a twin. She had everything she'd always wanted.

. . .

"I'm going to explode," muttered Molly, rubbing her stomach clockwise. Both girls were lying on the floor. Cookies—warm from the oven—had formed a very large percentage of their lunch. Possibly too large. Miri had heard somewhere that clockwise stomach-rubbing was good for digestion.

"Ugh." Miri stopped rubbing. "I think I heard wrong. Let's get up and do something."

"Like what? I'm too full to do much," sighed Molly.

Miri looked around the kitchen for ideas. Cookie, prowling the floor for possible traces of butter, stopped to watch her attentively. "I know. Let's make a movie. Let's make a movie about Cookie."

Their grandmother, who was under the impression that all her grandchildren were geniuses, had recently decided that Molly and Miri were brilliant artists. To help them express their amazingly hidden talents, she'd given them a camera, a good one. The girls had taken about five million pictures of themselves before they'd discovered that the camera also shot video, and then they'd annoyed everyone in the family by filming news shows about things like Mom fishing a mangled spoon out of the garbage disposal and Ray drooling as he slept, with whispered voice-overs commenting on the action.

"Okay." Molly heaved herself up and went in search of the camera. "We can call it *The Way the Cookie Crumbles.*"

But cats, they soon learned, make rotten actors. Cookie found the camera fascinating, so fascinating that she decided to sit down and stare at it.

"This is pretty boring," Molly said after a few minutes.

Miri tried to liven up the subject with her favorite toy, a crumpled napkin. Cookie took the napkin between her paws, bit it, and fell over.

"Jeez, forget it. You're fired," Molly told the kitten. Glancing around the familiar kitchen, her eyes stopped at the back door, the door that currently opened onto nothing. "I know," she said. She got to her feet. "Let's make a video of me walking out the back door. You know, like I think the porch is still there—and then, *zoop!* I disappear. It'll look like I've fallen down the rabbit hole. It'll be funny."

They decided it would be even funnier if Molly pretended to be superbusy and important. As Miri filmed, Molly rushed around the kitchen, frowning and shuffling papers and huffing about how late she was.

"Run," suggested Miri, giggling. "Run to the door and throw it open."

Molly looked at the clock, shrieked, and ran to

the door. She flung it open and dashed out, into empty air.

Where she stayed.

Not falling.

Not moving.

Standing.

On air.

. . .

In the tiny camera screen, Miri saw Molly turn slowly around, her eyes round with shock.

Very carefully, so as not to jar anything, Miri set the camera down.

Their eyes locked for a long moment. Neither of them moved.

Finally, Miri spoke quietly, "Is it—" She hesitated, not daring to say the word.

"I think so," Molly said, her voice thin. "I feel a floor. Under my feet, it feels like a floor." Cautiously, she lifted one foot and brought it down gently. "There's something there."

With as little movement as possible, Miri rose and tiptoed to the doorway. She looked down. She could see the ground below, a lumpy mixture of dirt and rocks and wood. She breathed out slowly and raised her eyes to her sister's.

Molly shook her head. "I know—I can see it, too—but still—I'm standing on something. I'm not, like, flying or anything."

Miri nodded, her skin prickling with excitement. *It's happening, it's happening, it's happening*, her mind sang, and she could feel her heart thumping—or maybe it was her stomach. Very slowly, she extended her flip-flop over the threshold. Something shifted; there was a small shudder, a loosening, and then, through the rubber sole, she felt a hard, flat, obvious surface. "It's a floor," she confirmed, feeling an enormous, elated smile spread across her face. "I didn't think we'd get it again," she whispered.

Joy flamed inside her. The magic had come back. For all the times she had assured Molly that it was possible, that magic might choose them again, she had told herself sternly that it wouldn't. Who could be so lucky? How could that lucky person be her? But now—she felt the shivery, electric thrill up her spine. Magic. For her and Molly.

"You said we might," Molly whispered.

"This house must be *full* of magic," Miri said in

wonderment. "You break off a little piece of house, and magic comes spilling out."

"Are you shaking?" asked Molly. "I'm shaking." She held out her hand. It was shaking.

Miri held out her own trembling hand to grasp her sister's and, strengthened, she turned to look at the world they had entered. Indians? she thought hopefully. No. Instead, there was the paint-peeling house, the tired grass, and the faint animal smells of the last journey through time. Molly's time. She'd last seen it in high summer. It was less dusty now and colder, and the trees that marked the edges of the backyard were turning gold, but aside from that, it was all very, very familiar. "We're back in 1935?" she whispered.

"Looks like it," Molly said.

Why? thought Miri with her first flash of worry. They had settled everything. They had finished with that time. She glanced to Molly and found her worry reflected in her sister's eyes.

"Why are we here?" Molly echoed her thoughts.

Miri shook her head weakly. She didn't know.

Suddenly, Molly's face cleared. "It's Grandma! She said I might see her again. She needs something."

Molly started toward the open door. "Grandma! It's me!"

"You're a disgrace!" cried a sharp voice from the kitchen.

Molly froze.

"Honestly, I'm going to lock you in the basement! See if I don't!"

Molly winced at Miri. Flo? she mouthed.

Miri nodded. Flo. Miri would have been perfectly happy to go the rest of her life without seeing Flo again. A sudden warmth circled Miri's bare ankle. She looked down to see Cookie, purring as she wound between the four available legs. The sight of the kitten weaving over open air made Miri feel seasick, and she quickly bent to scoop Cookie into her arms.

"A gentleman is paying me a call!" Flo's voice continued shrilly. "You can't drift around like— like—a crazy girl! I'll just die of embarrassment if he sees you!"

Molly shuddered. "Let's go around to the front," she murmured. "We can get to Grandma's room from the hall. I didn't come all the way back in time to listen to Flo yell at someone."

Miri nodded. "Me neither," she whispered. "And she's going to be yelling for a while, sounds like."

A light, chuckling voice bubbled from the kitchen. "You don't like my dress?"

Molly shot Miri a questioning look. Who was that?

"You ain't got no more sense than a horsefly!" snapped Flo. "That is a *nightgown*! Whatever are you thinking?"

Whoever it was, Miri and Molly felt sorry for her. The two girls began to edge away. It was cautious work, walking on an invisible floor, and they slid their feet over the unseen surface as quietly as they could, never quite taking a step, for there was no way to know when they would suddenly reach the porch's edge and tumble over it. Molly led the way, feeling blindly in front of herself with her foot. Sliding forward. Again. Again. Again—and there! An edge. "Stair?" she breathed, lowering her foot carefully—and yes! "Stair!" she said triumphantly.

"Shh!" warned Miri.

But it was too late. Instantly, the shrill voice squalled again, much closer, "Lord have mercy, there are two ragamuffins on the porch! Gypsies! They look like *Gypsies*! I swear, I can't keep things decent around here for one afternoon. Now, *get offa that porch, you tramps*!"

"Oh jeez!" hissed Molly, pulling Miri by the elbow as she scrambled down the invisible stairs. Cookie, gripped tight, squeaked in alarm.

"Head for the trees!" called Miri, staggering as she hit solid ground. But now they could run. And they did, leaping for the thick cluster of trees that rimmed the backyard. In less than a minute, they reached the safety of the woods and crouched, panting, behind a sturdy, comforting tree trunk.

"And don't you come back or I'll set the dog on you!" bellowed Flo from the porch, waving her fist.

"As if you even have a dog; you hate dogs—" muttered Molly. Suddenly, she stopped, her eyes widening.

"Oh my gosh," breathed Miri. While they had been running, the invisible back porch had become visible. It now stretched across the width of the house. It wasn't exactly the same porch as the one from Miri's time; it wasn't as wide and the stairs weren't in the same place, but it was definitely a porch. The house had regrown itself. Miri glanced to her right, down the long yard that bordered one side of the house. Yes, there was the barn, next to the old orchard that grew at the far edge of the property. In Miri's time, the barn was gone, its place taken by a tangled field of blackberries that had merged with the remains of the orchard. But Miri recognized what she saw: It was the same as the last time. They'd been dropped into 1935, into Molly's past. But *why*? thought Miri again. And another important question struck her: How are we going to get back?

Molly was standing stock-still, her eyes fixed on the porch. "That's not Flo." She took off her glasses, rubbed them with her dress, and put them back on.

"What?" Miri squinted through *her* glasses. Her eyesight was worse than Molly's, but she managed to make out a woman who was scrawny and knobby, like Flo. With a long, horsey face, like Flo's. But—

As Molly leaned forward for a better look, she was briefly exposed, resulting in an outraged holler. "I'm getting my shotgun right this minute!"

Miri yanked her sister back into the shadows. "What the heck are you doing?"

"Sorry. I was trying to see her better."

Once more, Miri squinted with all her might at the stranger's furious, flushed face. It was like searching for hidden pictures. Flo's long, bony jaw was there, but the pink cheeks were wrong. Something was wrong. "It's definitely her voice," she whispered. She hadn't seen Molly's aunt Flo very many times, but she had heard her. She had heard her raging at Molly: "Do you have to break everything you touch, you worthless child?" "I'll teach you about clumsy, miss!" Miri remembered the glad sound of Flo's voice, the ring of her slap against Molly's cheek, her quivering excitement as she announced she was planning to send Molly to the county home for orphans.

"I'd just as soon shoot you as look at you!" bleated the figure on the porch.

It was Flo's voice. It's was Flo's rotten temper. But this woman was too young, practically a girl. "Could it be Sissy?" Miri murmured. Sissy, Flo's daughter, was about the age of the porch girl.

Molly shook her head. "Not unless she got a lot uglier in a few months. And Sissy's hair isn't long enough to put up like that."

This was true. The young lady on the porch had a bun on the back of her head. "Not as pretty as Sissy," mumbled Miri. "Not as ugly as Flo."

"Weird."

As Cookie purred and the two girls stared at the faraway figure in perplexity, an odd idea began to grow in Miri's mind. She turned and looked again from the house to the yard, searching for clues. The backyard was untidy and overgrown, as usual. The barn? Weathered gray, it was just as it had been last time she'd seen it. Nearby, an assortment of chickens made their normal ruckus. 1935. Check and check. From her vantage point in the woods, Miri could see the back of the house, its side, and a hunk of the front yard. She inspected what she could see of it. Lawn, check. Elm tree, check. Wait. Her eyes darted back to the elm tree. In her own time, it stood regally in the middle of the circular lawn, shading the grass and house with its leafy canopy. Now it was shorter and smaller, though still lovely. But that wasn't what had caught her eye. She stared, narrowing and widening her eyes to focus them. In the web of gray branches, she glimpsed something odd. Something square. Something that seemed to be a small structure. It looked like—a tree house? "Mols," she said quietly. "Look at the elm. Is that a tree house?"

Molly looked. After a moment, she said wonderingly, "Why would Sissy put up a tree house?"

"It's not 1935," Miri said.

Molly's eyes darted to her face and back to the tree. "Not 1935?"

"It's longer ago," Miri said. "That's Flo, but—"

"Younger!" cried Molly. "That's it! She's young!" She whirled around. The horsey woman, her long chin in the air, was marching back inside. "Quick! Look at the dress! What year?"

Pink. Halfway between the ankle and the knee. "Well," said Miri doubtfully, "I guess it's not hoop-skirt time."

Molly lifted an eyebrow. "Good work, Sherlock. How old do you figure she is?"

Miri wasn't very good at that, either. "Twenty? Maybe twenty-five? I don't know."

"Yeah, that's what I think, too." Molly fell silent then, her eyes circling the white house, the red and gold trees, the nearly empty beds of vegetables, the faraway elm.

"What?" asked Miri, watching her.

Molly's gray eyes were shadowy as they turned back to Miri. "Why are we here?"

Miri shook her head. She didn't know.

"You always say that magic doesn't waste its . . . its strength, or whatever you want to call it, on fun. You say that if magic happens, it's for a reason."

"That's what your grandma said," Miri broke in.

"Yeah, I know," said Molly. " 'Magic is just a way of setting things right.' So what year is it, and what are we supposed to do?"

"I don't know. Maybe—" She broke off as a door slammed.

All of them, Cookie included, tensed to run. Especially, Miri thought, if Flo reappeared with a shotgun in her hands.

But it wasn't Flo.

A very pretty teenage girl floated across the porch and down the stairs. Miri had always thought that was an authorish way of saying that someone was graceful, because, obviously, nobody floated except in water. But this girl seemed to. She seemed to hover ever so slightly above the surface of the stairs as she descended. How the heck does she do that? wondered Miri, scrutinizing the girl's feet. No, she wasn't floating; she was walking like a regular person. Miri could see the tips of her shoes touch the wood. But she moved so lightly, her long, dark hair trailing behind her. Miri watched in admiring fascination as the girl skimmed over the stairs that Miri and Molly had so recently stumbled down and then made quickly for the very cluster of trees where they were hiding.

Molly and Miri drew deeper into the shadows, but they didn't run. As the girl came closer, Miri noticed her bright, thick-lashed eyes and her eager smile. She also noticed that the girl was wearing a nightgown. This was the one Flo had been yelling at in the kitchen. Miri relaxed. Any enemy of Flo's was a friend of theirs.

The unknown girl came to a halt and peered uncertainly into the veil of leaves. After a moment, she said softly, "If you're still there, would you please come out? I won't hurt you or tell anyone about you."

Shifting Cookie into the crook of her arm, Miri nudged Molly. Should we? Molly didn't respond.

"Please?" coaxed the girl.

Without warning, Molly stumbled forward. Miri, startled, followed.

The girl smiled happily. "Well, hello!" she said.

There was a pause. "Are you-all hungry? I can get you some bread and butter. Or something else, anything you'd prefer. I don't know what Gypsies like," she added.

Miri waited for Molly to answer, but she didn't. "We're not exactly Gypsies," explained Miri hesitantly, hoping the girl wouldn't ask her who, then, they were.

Her face fell. "Really? Blast!" Then she looked worried again. "Excuse me. I'm sure you're very nice anyway. It's just that I've been searching for Gypsies for years." Her eyes ran over Miri's and Molly's clothes. "You *sure* you're not Gypsies?"

There was something about her that made Miri want to make her happy. "Well," she wavered, glancing down at her jeans and T-shirt. "Maybe we are, in a way."

The girl looked positively thrilled. "That's what I thought! Now, you mustn't fret about me—I won't tell a soul! I'm not like her." She tipped her head toward the porch. "I just need to learn how to tell fortunes." She gave Miri and Molly a dazzling smile and leaned forward confidingly. "See, ever since I was little, I wanted to run off and join the circus. You know, for adventure?" She nodded enthusiastically, and Miri, liking her, nodded back. "Don't you think I'd be a good fortune-teller? I look like one in this nightgown, for sure. But—I don't know how to do it. Tell fortunes, I mean," she added hurriedly. "Which is a hitch. For a fortune-teller. So"—she smiled hopefully at Miri and Molly—"will you teach me?"

"How old are you?" blurted Molly in an odd, choked voice.

Miri glanced at her sister. It was sort of a rude question, in her opinion. Or maybe not. She couldn't tell if the girl was old enough to make it a rude question.

The girl didn't seem offended. "I'm seven*teen*!" she exclaimed. "I know it's awful old to be running off to the circus, but"—she spread her hands out helplessly—"it's a lifelong dream, and here you are, Gypsies. I don't meet so many Gypsies that I can let you slip through my fingers." She smiled. "Do you tell the cards?" she asked, turning to Molly. "Or read palms?" She laughed, thrusting out her palm. "What does my future hold?"

Molly recoiled as if the girl had tried to hit

her. "Molly?" asked Miri, alarmed. "What's the matter?"

Molly didn't answer. She backed away fearfully.

The girl looked concerned. "You needn't worry," she said. "I know I look crazy, but I'm not. Really." Her chuckle came, warm and bubbling. "I'm only dressed like this to aggravate Flo—that's the one who was hollering at you. She's got a caller coming, and I'm ruining her good impression." She smiled mischievously and fluffed her long gown. "But it's awful comfortable. I might just keep on wearing them. People already think I'm a little peculiar."

"It looks good on you," said Miri.

"Not exactly ladylike." The girl smiled.

"Well," said Miri, looking down, "same here."

"Oh," the girl said airily. "Gypsies can get away with anything. Now, won't you please tell my fortune? I can pay you, I certainly can. If you promise not to stir a step, I can just run right inside and get my glove box. That's where I keep my—"

"What year is it?" demanded Molly. Miri goggled at her sister; why was she being so strange? She seemed almost angry. Usually, Molly was the friendly one, the chatty one—she talked to anyone, including grumpy bus drivers and strict teachers—but now, for some reason, she had turned abrupt and rude.

The girl giggled. "Law, you *must* be Gypsies. 1918." For the first time, her eyes fell on Cookie, draped snoozily in the crook of Miri's arm. "Ooh, look at that little darling." She reached to rub the kitten's downy fur, causing an explosion of purring.

"You want to hold her?" asked Miri.

"Can I?"

In answer, Miri transferred Cookie into the girl's arms.

"I just love cats," the girl confided. "I used to have one named Larimer—don't ask me why—he was just the smartest thing—"

"We have to go!" blurted Molly. "Now." She whirled around to Miri. "We have to go, right? We're late. Come on." She turned and walked swiftly away through the trees.

"Molly!" cried Miri, scandalized by her sister's behavior. "Sorry," she apologized to the girl.

Her eyes, hurt, were on Molly's receding back. "Guess she thinks I'm peculiar, too," she murmured. "Well. Here." She returned Cookie to Miri's arm.

Miri tried to make up for Molly's bad manners. "I guess I have to go. Um, maybe we'll see you later."

The girl nodded sadly. "Yes, of course. Delightful to make your acquaintance."

⌁ CHAPTER ⌁

4

INSIDE THE BARN, Miri tried again. "Just tell me."

Molly lifted her face from her hands, shook her head miserably, and dropped her face into her hands once more.

The brief glimpse was not heartening. Miri had never seen Molly so defeated. Molly, the brave, the daring, the confident. Molly, who gritted her teeth and got on with it. Molly, whose nerves of steel Miri envied every day of her life—suddenly, for no reason Miri could see, she was overcome. Horst, the tyrant of her former life, had done everything he could to break her, but the worst Horst could dish up had only made Molly more rebellious and defiant. Never despairing. For the twentieth time, Miri reviewed the events of the previous hour, trying to find the source of her sister's trouble. 1918. Was there something the matter with it? Nothing came to mind. Was there something bad about fortune-telling . . . ?

As she nosed among empty stalls and pieces of old machinery, Cookie was encountering a variety of exciting odors: hay, rust, cows, soil, and—ah!—the alluring fragrance of mice! Just in time for lunch! Cookie pursued the mousy perfume into a corner, where she crouched, preparing her attack. A low growl rattled in her throat, and she leaped forward ferociously to do battle with a mouse, which turned out to be her own tail. Miri nudged Molly. "Look."

Molly glanced up and nodded dully.

"It's better if we do stuff together, Mols. Just tell me."

Molly looked at her.

"How terrible can it be?"

Silence.

"I don't get it!" Miri broke out. "She was just a nice girl. So what?"

Molly's voice was low. "You don't know who she was?"

It was the first thing she'd said in almost an hour, and Miri jumped at it. "How would I know? She could be anyone! She could be a neighbor! She could be a relative! Heck, she could be Flo's sister, for all I know!" Suddenly, she stopped, and her hand flew to her mouth. Flo's sister. Flo's sister was— "Your mother," she whispered. "She's your mother. Oh gosh. I get it."

Miri didn't know much about Molly's mother, her first mother. Her name was—Miri hunted through her memory and found it—Maudie. And she was dead. By the time Miri had met Molly in 1935, Maudie had been dead a long time. That's all Miri knew.

Molly nodded, her mouth folded tight and her eyes filled with tears. At the sight of her tears, Miri began to chew on her knuckle. Molly didn't cry very often. Even when she dropped the bathroom scale on her toe, she didn't cry. But now her thick eyelashes were beaded, and Miri felt her own throat grow tight in sympathy. "I guess you haven't seen her in a long time, huh?"

Molly rubbed her eyes with her sleeve. "I've never seen her."

"Never?" Miri slipped her hand around Molly's. "Were you little when she—um—" She didn't want to say it. Saying it made it real.

"She died when I was born," said Molly.

"Ohh." Miri grimaced. That was bad.

"Yeah. My fault." Molly blew out a long breath.

Miri couldn't allow that. "No! Don't think that! You didn't do it!"

Molly looked haunted. "Yes, I did. There's no getting around it. She died when she had me."

Miri couldn't think of anything comforting to say. That nice girl was going to die. It hurt to think about it.

"She wanted to know her fortune," Molly whispered. "It's a pretty bad fortune."

Miri nodded. It was a pretty bad fortune.

"She seemed nice, didn't she?" Molly asked.

"Really nice. And funny, too. You look like her."

Molly shook her head. "No. She's beautiful."

"Well, you look like her, and you're pretty pretty now. So you'll probably be beautiful when you're seventeen."

"Seventeen," repeated Molly. "She's only got six years to live. A little more than six years."

"She dies when she's twenty-three?" Miri asked unhappily. "Only twenty-three?" That was young. Young to have a baby. Very young to die.

Molly looked across the hayloft, blinking rapidly.

"Listen," urged Miri. "Listen, let's"—she searched for something, anything to make it better"—let's go ask your grandma!" The words fell out of her mouth before she knew she was going to say them, but instantly, she knew she was right. Grandma May knew magic inside and out. She'd have an idea, maybe even a solution. "Maybe there's something we can do!" She gave Molly's shoulder a squeeze. "I mean, think about it—what do we know for sure? We know that magic is a way of setting things right. Right?" she prodded, and Molly nodded. "So maybe we're here to do something for your—your mother." She tripped over the word. It sounded wrong when it didn't mean *their* mother. "It's possible, anyway."

Molly whirled around. "Why, sure!" she cried, her tear-damp face brightening. "Of course! You're totally right! That's what we're here for!" She shook her head, wondering at herself. "I don't know why I didn't think of it before. I mean, it's obvious, right? Grandma knows *everything*! She's magic herself!

She's bound to have a solution. My gosh, I can't believe I wasted all this time!" Filled with new purpose, Molly jumped to her feet. "Come on. Grab Cookie. Let's go."

. . .

The distance between the barn and the house was at least fifty miles. That's what it looked like to Miri, anyway. She paused beside the barn, eyeing the wide lawn and trying not to think about Flo and her shotgun.

The two girls had edged out the barn door and gone toward the corner nearest the house. Their appearance caused pandemonium among the chickens, but then, everything caused pandemonium among chickens. They sidled past the pigs, who watched them with utter boredom, and a dignified goose, who decided that they weren't worth biting. Now, though, they had arrived at the point of no return: To get to Molly's grandmother, inside the house, they had to cross the open lawn.

Molly was undaunted. In fact, she was fizzing with determination. "Just aim for those rhododendrons there under the window," she whispered, pointing to a large window on the side of the house, which Miri recognized as belonging to the living room. "The bushes will cover us all the way from that side around to the front stairs."

"Okay." Cookie squirmed, and Miri clutched her firmly. "Let's go on the count of three," she whispered, trying to work up her nerve.

Molly turned, and Miri caught a flash of her usual fearless smile. "Three," she whispered, and sprinted toward the house.

"Molly!" groaned Miri in an undertone, and raced after her, hoping Flo was far away.

Seconds later, she was ducking into the rhododendron bushes. They had no flowers now, in the fall, but their leaves grew thick and full against the sides of the house, and as Molly had predicted, the two of them were well hidden within. Molly crept forward, taking the lead, and Miri followed, concentrating on careful, silent steps.

Cookie squirmed again, desperate to free herself, to leap into this paradise of branches and *climb*! Wildly, she wiggled against the arm that imprisoned her, only to have it clamp around her even more tightly. Branch after tempting branch flashed by, unclimbed, and Cookie decided that the time had come to deploy the ultimate weapon. She dug her claws into the arm.

"Yow!" squeaked Miri, and tripped over a root. She fell with a crash into a tangle of branches. The noise was astounding, even without the shriek that she managed to keep bottled up inside her.

Molly pulled her quickly from the thicket to crouch against the house. Are you okay? she mouthed. Miri nodded, trying to ignore a stinging something on her forehead, but there was no time to investigate, because a window above them rose with a rumble. They froze as a girlish voice said, "Why, it must've been some awful *animal* of my sister's."

"Didn't know you had a sister." A deep man's voice moved toward the window.

"Oh my, *yes*!" tinkled the girl. Miri and Molly shared questioning looks. Could this be Flo? It sounded like her, but with frosting. "She's just a *child*, of course. And she's wild about animals, 'specially cats—and pigs, too, if you can believe that. She talks to them just like they're *people*. Isn't that crazy?"

Miri could almost see Flo shaking her head in aren't-children-silly amazement.

"I'm real fond of pigs myself," the man said.

"Nobody gives them any credit, but think of it—they spend their lives eating and rolling in the mud. They don't work and they don't fight. That's pretty smart in my book."

Flo burbled out a lot of fake-sounding giggles. "Aren't you a card!" she trilled. Miri and Molly rolled their eyes at the idea of Flo trying to be sweet. "Now, I want to show you something I just *know* you'll be interested in, a military man like you!" Her voice faded as she moved away.

"I'm not a military man anymore," he called after her. There was no answer, and Miri and Molly heard him sigh. They smiled at each other. The poor guy, stuck with Flo.

Back she came, *tap, tap, tap*. "My grandfather's medals, from the War Between the States—"

"We call it the Civil War," interrupted the man drily.

Giggle, titter. "You Yankees! Anyway, see, he got the Southern Cross—that's this here."

Molly batted her eyelashes at Miri, who batted hers back.

"Very nice," muttered the man.

"But here's what's *interesting*," enthused Flo. "Look at this!"

There was a silence. "From Lee," the man said. This time he did sound a little interested.

"*Yes.* General Robert E. Lee, commander in chief—see, he signed it here. See?" Miri could picture Flo shoving whatever it was in the man's face. "It's a safe-conduct. See? 'Bearer must in no way and for no purpose be detained from the pursuit of his duties. Let neither his costume nor his demeanor cause his arrest. He is in my service. General R. E. Lee.' *Now*," cried Flo, "don't *you* think that means my granddaddy was a *spy*?"

"Well," said the man slowly, "could be. Looks like he was up to some kind of mischief for the Confederacy, anyway."

"Ooh, it just makes me *shiver* to think of it," squealed Flo.

Miri tossed imaginary curls about as Molly waved an imaginary fan and smiled coyly. Miri heaved a silent but passionate sigh. Molly indicated that she might throw up any second. They found themselves so entertaining that they missed the man's answer.

Flo's voice drifted out: "—for some tea and cookies. I baked them special for you."

Molly and Miri gave identical guilty starts. Cookie!

Where was she? As the window above them was drawn down, they twisted about, hunting for a little white kitten among the branches. "She must have jumped away when I tripped," whispered Miri, peering through the leaves. "Cookie!" she whisper-shouted.

"There!" said Molly with relief, pointing. And there was Cookie, a tiny lion in the underbrush, her eyes gleaming, her tail stiff, preparing an attack on a bird that pecked in the nearby dirt.

"Cookie!" Miri whispered, reaching for her.

Alarmed by the crackling of leaves, Cookie she took a wild, spitting lunge at her prey. The bird flew off in annoyance.

"Here, kitty!" called Miri in a strangled whisper as Cookie, embarrassed by her failure, pretended to be deeply interested in the cleanliness of her leg. "Here, kitty!"

Cookie glanced at her and then trotted out of the rhododendrons toward the front stairs. She felt a nap coming on. There was sure to be comfortable spot on the porch.

"Oh heck," sighed Miri. "Now we have to go get her."

Molly assessed the situation like a general. "Okay," she said, half to herself. "Okay. No problem. We'll just go up the stairs, grab her off the porch, and just sort of tiptoe in the front door."

"But Flo's in the living room," Miri reminded her.

"Oh. Right. Okay, once we have Cookie, we'll zip around to the back and go through the kitchen to Grandma's room. And if Grandma's not in there, we'll just—just—*find* her. Right?"

"Right," said Miri, trying and failing to sound confident. If Flo caught them, what then?

"We can't let Flo stop us," said Molly fiercely, as if she'd read Miri's mind. "We need to talk to Grandma."

Once again, they set out through the maze of branches—Miri extra careful this time—and sidled around the posts that marked the stairs. Miri noticed that the stairs were painted white. In her time, they were green. White looked better, she thought. Maybe we should repaint ours. She shook the thought away. Focus!

Cookie eyed the approaching enemy and decided on a strategic retreat. She padded deeper into the porch, where the wicker chairs were arranged in a circle, and jumped up on a rocking chair.

Miri and Molly glared at the kitten in silent exasperation and tiptoed toward the rocker. Molly reached out, ready to scoop.

Cookie jumped to the floor.

"Dang!" muttered Molly as Cookie skittered through her fingers.

"I've got her!" puffed Miri, lunging.

"It's the *Gypsies*!" shrieked Flo dramatically, appearing on the porch.

Startled, Miri glanced up, and Cookie slithered from her grip. "Cu-*rap*!" she yelled.

"Those are Gypsies?" inquired the voice of Mr. Whoever-he-was, from the doorway. "They don't look like Gypsies."

"They're Gypsy tramps," wailed Flo. "Look at them!"

"Oh, Flo, shut *up*!" panted Molly, her eyes on Cookie's retreating behind. "Gotcha!" she cried.

Cookie slid triumphantly through Molly's fingers and scanned the porch for another escape hatch. Aha! The door!

"How do you know my name, you nasty thing?" squalled Flo.

"She's heading inside!" called Miri.

"I've got her," the man said calmly, bending down. But Cookie darted around him and galloped over the threshold. The man straightened. "Then again, maybe I don't." He grinned.

"Come back, you devil-kitty!" said Miri.

"Saints alive!" squealed Flo. "The cat's possessed!"

"Jeez, Flo, just calm down!" Miri said irritably, moving after the kitten. She was almost inside when she realized that Molly wasn't next to her. "Molly!" she called, turning back. "Come on!"

Molly didn't move. She stood frozen, her eyes glued to the man beside Flo, the color draining from her face. Miri spun to him, but he wasn't doing anything frightening that she could see. He was smiling, almost laughing, while Flo, red-faced from yelling, continued to rant about Gypsies and devils. He was a tall man, very tanned, and one of his hands was wrapped in a white bandage. That's why he couldn't catch Cookie, thought Miri briefly. She called again, "Molly!"

Molly didn't move.

What had happened to her? Miri began to panic. "Mols! Come on! Snap out of it!"

"That's it!" shrieked Flo. "I'm getting my shotgun!"

The man really did laugh at that. "Never fear, Miss Gliscoe! I will protect you from these dangerous criminals."

Flo didn't seem to understand that he was joking. "You're so brave," she whimpered, edging close to him. "I'm awful frightened."

"Move, Molly. Please," begged Miri, casting a desperate look at the kitten prancing down the hallway.

Molly took a step, but it was in the wrong direction, and Miri saw the dizzy sway of her shoulders. "Molly!" she cried, and charged for her, grabbing her hand and yanking her toward the hallway. "Hang in there. We'll just get Cookie—that's all, and then we'll find your—"

"Molly?" A light voice seemed to still the frenzy around them, and Molly's white face seemed to flicker back to life. "Molly, sweetheart?" And there, in the hallway, was May, much younger than before, her brilliant blue eyes sparkling with astonishment.

"Oh, Grandma," Molly gasped. She stumbled toward the small figure, spilling words as she went. "Grandma, what am I supposed to—"

Grandma May took a step backward, lifting a

hand to ward Molly off. "Don't!" she cried. "Don't come in!"

But it was too late. Miri and Molly were already stepping over the threshold when they heard her words. There was a shudder, as though every dimension that held them turned, individually, in a separate direction. "Grandma!" Molly cried, straining to reach her grandmother's hand. "No! Not yet!"

"Well, okay, if you say so," said Mom. She stopped in the hall, a laundry basket in her hands, eyeing her daughters questioningly. "But the boys got fake blood all over their jeans, so I'm doing a load." She glanced at the kitten in Miri's arms. "You fed her, didn't you?"

Miri looked down, surprised. She didn't know how or when she'd managed to pick up Cookie. She nodded.

Her mother frowned. "Are you all right? You both look a little pale."

"We're fine," croaked Miri. She cleared her throat. "We're great."

Molly nodded woodenly.

Mom wasn't satisfied. "You sound hoarse, too," she said. "Do you want some tea?"

"Sure. Tea," Miri said, and her mother went toward the kitchen. Without a word, Molly backed up to the wall and slid downward. Miri watched her in silence. After a moment, she set Cookie into her sister's lap and watched as the kitten kneaded Molly's leg into a suitable resting place. Molly stared straight ahead, unmoving.

Miri let out a long breath. "That was your dad, wasn't it?"

Molly nodded.

❖ CHAPTER ❖

5

"AND THEN THERE WAS THIS OTHER GUY, he was all olden—" Ray paused to swallow, and Robbie took over enthusiastically.

"And he says something all heroic, like 'Victory or heaven awaits us, boys!' and then we're supposed to run across the field after him."

"I did!" said Ray through a huge wad of pasta.

"So did I," protested Robbie.

"*Pssht*," sneered Ray. "You were like, 'After *you*, my dear Alphonse.' And—oh, man"—he turned gleefully to their father—"did you see the guy who got blown up?"

Miri looked up from her plate. "For real?"

Ray rolled his eyes. "Don't be derpy. It was a

reenactment! Duh! But he had blood pellets or something, and, whoa, it looked like half his brains were falling out!"

Mom glanced worriedly at Nell and Nora. "Did you learn *any* history at all?" she asked.

Robbie looked at Ray and frowned. "It was the Battle of Cedar Creek," he said. "Right?"

"Sheridan," mumbled Molly without knowing she had done so.

Her brothers turned on her, outraged. "How do you know that?" demanded Ray.

She looked up, startled. "What? Oh. I was guessing. Am I right?"

Robbie scowled at her, and, not to be entirely upstaged, Ray added, "Mr. Emory was him. General Sheridan. He rode a horse and everything, and when this other guy said we had to retreat, he came up with his sword out and totally screamed"—Ray's screech made them all jump—"'If you love your country, come up to the front! Come up to the front, dammit!'" He grinned at his mother. "Hey, it's historic swearing."

Robbie guffawed. "Yeah, there was this guy, he said this one I never heard before—"

"That's not exactly the kind of history I was hoping for," interrupted their mother. "What happened after Mr. Emory screamed?"

"Oh," said Ray with his mouth full, "we turned around and ran back and fought the gray guys."

"You didn't fight for real, did you?" asked Miri. It sounded terrible, this reenactment thing.

Robbie shook his head. "Mostly we'd sort of run at each other and then a gray guy would say, 'I got you, you're dead,' and I'd say 'No way,' and run in the other direction."

"But anyway," continued Ray. "We won."

"Mommy got us ice cream," said Nell.

"Mr. Emory said we could keep the uniforms until next week. There's another one next Saturday," said Ray.

Mom and Dad exchanged looks. "You liked it that much?" asked Dad.

"Sure," said Ray. "It's hecka fun."

"Why?" asked Mom.

"It's like a video game," he explained.

. . .

Steamy and flushed from her shower, Miri came into the bedroom she shared with Molly. It was small, their room, and cozy, wallpapered with a pattern of pink roses. Molly and Miri had decided, at the beginning of their twinhood, that they were going to be neat and tidy. They were going to put things away where they belonged. They were going to be organized and artistic at the same time. Their room was going to look like a magazine room. That had lasted about a week and a half. It was funny, Miri thought. Most people, if they had to bet, would guess that she, Miri, the dreamier, less practical one, would be the messier of the two. But she wasn't. Miri liked to make arrangements and setups. Her collection of sea glass, for instance, was laid out in a spiral of colors: green, white, brown, blue, and, at the center, the extremely rare red. It glowed in the light, and the prettiness of it made Miri happy. Molly cared less about how things looked. Every once in a while, she would go on an organizing spree, but most of the time, she was focused on completing projects, on getting things done, and if that meant sweeping everything from the desk onto the floor to make more room, that was what she would do.

Now, standing at her dresser, Miri absently put some hair clips back into their tiny drawer and gave Molly a quick sideways glance. There she was, at the desk, bent over a book. Homework. Miri got into her pj's and brushed her hair. Putting on her glasses, she leaned into the mirror, fingering the rhododendron scrape on her forehead. It was long and crooked and purplish. It would be a great scar, Miri thought. She could say she'd received it in a duel. "Hey, Molly, you think I'm going to get a scar?"

Molly twitched. "What?"

"Sorry," said Miri, subdued. "Never mind." She watched Molly's reflection, her stillness, her unblinking eyes. Slowly, Miri continued to brush her hair, watching. Molly didn't move. "What homework are you doing?" she asked.

"What? Oh. Math," said Molly.

Miri frowned. "Pretty weird that you've got your Spanish book in front of you then."

Molly looked down at her book. "Oh."

There was a long silence.

Miri tried again. "How'd you know about that Meridan guy?"

After a moment, Molly frowned. "What?"

"That guy. Come up if you love your country," said Miri. "The general. You know."

"Sheridan," said Molly, still not looking up. "It's

from before. The Civil War was still a big deal in 1935. Everyone knew that stuff. There were still people around who'd been in it."

Ugh. Before. So much for changing the subject. Miri decided to go for it, "Molly, what're you thinking? I mean, I know you're worrying, because—because I know, but there's nothing you can *do*." She frowned at the back of Molly's head. "Even if we could go back, through the kitchen door like today, what would you do? I mean, there's no way for you to stop it or fix—" She broke off. It occurred to her that there *was* one way to fix it. Maudie would remain alive if Molly were never born. Miri glanced incredulously at the back of Molly's head. "You're not thinking that you shouldn't be born, are you?"

Molly shifted in her chair.

"Molly, that's totally crazy. You can't stop yourself from existing, because you *do* exist, so you have to exist." Miri realized she was arguing herself into a corner, but she kept going. "You can't just subtract yourself from the world. You're already here!"

Molly said softly, "I wasn't always here. You know that. I was added. I could be subtracted."

"No, you couldn't!"

"Magic is just a way of setting things right," Molly continued as if Miri hadn't spoken. "Why would magic have sent us back to 1918 today unless I'm supposed to save Maudie?"

"That wouldn't be setting anything right!" Miri yelled. "That wouldn't make anything better! That would make things a lot, lot worse!"

"Not for Maudie. Not for my dad," said Molly.

"What're you going to do, kidnap her and take her away so she never meets him?" Molly looked quickly away, out the window, and Miri realized that her guess had come fairly close to the truth. "You can't! That's crazy!" she snapped, rubbing at the tears that were leaking out from under her glasses.

Molly turned to look at her, and Miri saw her bite her lip. "I guess you're right," she said. "You're probably right. It's a stupid idea." She blinked. "Don't worry about it."

Miri swiped at her cheeks angrily. "Don't worry about it, she says. Don't worry that you want to go back in time and stop yourself from being born. Okay, I won't worry about it. I'll just think about other important things like, like"—she looked around the room wildly—"like where my pink socks are, because I really, really care about my pink socks!" She was ranting—she knew she was, but she couldn't seem to stop.

"They're under your mattress."

"No, they aren't!" huffed Miri.

"Yes, they are. I've been looking at them for weeks," Molly said.

"Well! You should have told me!" yelled Miri. She marched to the bunk bed and haughtily reached under her mattress. Just as Molly said, her socks were wedged between the mattress and the boards that held her bunk up. *"Humph!"* she sniffed, yanking them out.

"Don't be mad," Molly begged. "Come on, Miri, please?"

Miri paused uncertainly. She knew she was only mad so she wouldn't have to be sad and scared. She glanced at her sister. "You're not going to do it, right?"

Molly shook her head. "It was a stupid idea," she repeated.

Miri peered at her. She couldn't tell whether Molly was telling the truth or saying what she thought Miri wanted to hear. It was unlike Molly to change her mind so easily, to be so un-stubborn. "Molly," she began, "come on. Tell me. What are you going to do?"

Molly's eyes slid away from hers. "I told you. I'm not going to do anything." There was a pause. "Let's just go to bed."

Miri watched her, feeling excluded. It was a feeling she knew well; it was what she'd felt before, for years, when she was the sole only between two sets of twins. It was hungry, this feeling, and it hurt, and she had been free of it since Molly had come to live in her time. But here it was again: the lonely feeling of caring more than the other person did. "Fine," she said slowly.

"It's been a long day," Molly said, turning away.

At the beginning of it, I was happy, thought Miri. I thought we both were. But maybe it was just me. She didn't say it. In silence, she climbed the ladder to her bed and turned off the light. In the dark, she craned her neck to find the moon in the round window. It wasn't there. "We can switch bunks if you want," Miri offered. "It's okay with me."

Molly's voice came after a moment. "That's all right," she said. "It's fine the way it is."

"Okay. If you're sure," said Miri. She stared into the empty black, wishing, for the first time in her life, that there were no such thing as magic.

. . .

Unsleeping. That's what it should be called, Miri thought. Unsleeping—when your mind refuses to stop thinking. Beneath her came the sound of Molly shifting restlessly. Unsleeping.

Kicking free of her hot sheets, Miri found her glasses and looked at the clock. It was only eleven thirty. So many hours to go.

Below, Molly's bed creaked as she sat up. "I can't sleep," she said.

"Me neither."

"I'm going to go find Mom."

"Me too."

They slid out of bed and went down their narrow stairway. The big house was quiet, but reassuring lamplight glowed in the living room. Their mother looked up from her book as they entered. "Can't sleep?"

They nodded.

"Okay." Mom shifted to the middle of the couch

and patted the pillows beside her. "One on each side."

"You're never mad when we get up at night," said Molly, settling in.

Mom smiled and smoothed a wisp of hair from her forehead. "That's because I always miss you guys after you go to bed." She dropped a kiss on the top of Molly's head. "Isn't that nutty?"

Miri snuggled into her mother's other side. "Mom sandwich," she murmured, and heard her mother smile. Minutes slipped by quietly; Miri listened to Molly's breathing and her mother's, the efficient ticking of the clock in the hall.

"Mom?" It was Robbie. In the dim light, his blue eyes were huge.

"You too?" said Mom. She smiled at him and reached around Miri to toss a pillow on the floor. He sat, edging close to her knee. "Today was a little tough, huh?" Mom asked softly.

Robbie nodded. "I keep thinking about what the real thing must've been like."

"War, you mean?" asked Mom.

"Yeah."

"Bad," she said. "Awful."

"I don't see how they could do it. Fight like that, I mean," said Robbie. "I couldn't. Not for real." He stared moodily at the rug.

Then the quiet resumed and stretched on in the golden pool of light. Miri leaned forward: Molly's eyes were closed, her head nestled in the curve of Mom's arm, at peace and easy. No, Miri thought, she won't leave. We're her family. She would never leave Mom. Or me. Or all of us.

Everything will be okay, she thought.

Everything will be—

She was asleep.

. . .

Bright day. Miri could tell without opening her eyes that her bedroom was flooded with sun. She curled and then stretched, a long, unfolding stretch that must have added at least an inch to her height. "Molly?"

No answer, and suddenly, the day before came rushing back to her.

"Mols?" Miri draped her head over the side of the bunk to peer into the bed below. It was empty and comforter-tossed.

She's just downstairs, Miri told herself. Just downstairs, eating breakfast, chomp, chomp, have some toast. She realized that she was talking to herself the way you do when you're pretending you're not scared—"There's nothing outside that window, not a thing, just some trees, some good old trees." Still, Miri insisted, she is downstairs. Where else would she be? *1918*, said her enemy brain. Shut up, she told it. Molly wouldn't do that. *Yes, she would, to set things right. It's exactly the kind of thing she'd do.* Miri threw off her comforter and went down the ladder in the Mom-disapproved fastest possible way, which was a backward leap. She didn't notice she was saying Molly's name until she slammed into the kitchen. "Molly, Molly, Molly—"

And there she was, at the kitchen table. She looked up at Miri. "Hi."

"Hi!" Miri bellowed in relief.

"Are you *trying* to wake up everyone in the house?" asked her father. "If so, you're doing a great job." He frowned at her as she collapsed limply into a chair beside Molly. "Up half the night," he muttered, turning back to his toolbox, open on the counter, "and some of us have work to do." Mutter, mutter, mutter.

"What're you doing?" asked Miri to distract him from his muttering.

He rattled something in the toolbox. "Gotta board up that door." He jerked his head at the open back door. "So you kids don't forget and go flying out of it. Or leave it open so the kitten falls out—" He fell silent, intent on nails, and then resumed. "But I can't start hammering until your mama wakes up. Or nine o'clock, whichever comes first. Is this three inches?" He held up a nail.

"Could be," said Miri, cheerful now that Molly was found. She tapped her spoon on the table. "No glasses. Can't see a thing."

"It's three and a quarter," said a hearty voice. Ollie's head appeared to be resting on the door's threshold.

"Ollie!" said Dad, taking a surprised step back. "Oh. You're standing on a ladder."

"Naw," Ollie chortled, "I grew in the night." He peered into the kitchen. "I'm going to get to work measuring for the posts." He waved his hand behind him, but his eyes were glued to the kitchen ceiling. "I think maybe you got some rot up there. See how it's peeling?"

Dad looked at the ceiling. "One thing at a time."

"If you say so," Ollie said. He gave the ceiling a longing look and disappeared from view.

"That guy's crazy about rot," Miri whispered.

"Yeah," Molly said vaguely.

"I got scared you'd gone back," Miri confided, hoping for an indignant denial.

Molly nodded.

Miri pressed, "Even though I know you wouldn't."

Molly shook her head, but she didn't look Miri in the eye.

"You wouldn't, would you?" demanded Miri.

"No. Course not," Molly said. "And anyway, Dad's about to board up the door. In a few minutes, I wouldn't be able to get back even if I wanted to."

Miri gave her a sharp glance. Who was she kidding? Molly wasn't a person who could be stopped by anything so paltry as a few boards. She was faking.

∽ CHAPTER ∾

6

WAS SHE FAKING? For roughly the millionth time that week, Miri wondered.

"Waaay back!" called Ray. "To the driveway!"

"You're dreaming!" hollered Molly. She took one step back. "You'll *maybe* get it to the tree."

They were playing lettuce-ball, the only fun part of grocery shopping. Basically, it was football with heads of lettuce, but they weren't allowed to ruin the lettuce, so it was mostly passing and yelling.

Even though lettuce-ball was the only sport she truly enjoyed, Miri wasn't having a good time. She couldn't keep her mind on the game. She was too busy watching Molly from the corner of her eye, trying to read her mind. Was she planning to go back in time to save Maudie? Was she planning to erase herself from Miri's life? What was she thinking? Oops—lettuce sailed past Miri's shoulder, and Nora caught it, shrieking with excitement. "I got it! I got it!"

Nora's triumph didn't last long. Molly raced forward to scoop her and her lettuce up and head for the goal (lettuce-ball was also like soccer). "She scores!" she screamed over her shoulder as she ran.

"No, she doesn't!" shouted Robbie, chasing her down.

Miri stood in the shade of the elm tree, watching Molly. No. She'd never do it. Look how much fun she was having. She'd never play around like that if she was leaving. She'd be tense and worried, or maybe that's just how Miri herself would be— "Ow!" This time, the lettuce hit her on the forehead.

Miri had been repeating versions of this argument all week long. Each day, she and Molly went to school, came home on the bus, played with Cookie, did their homework, read, went to bed, and did everything they normally did. Except that it wasn't normal.

The most un-normal part was not talking about it. Miri had tried. In the middle of finding the volume of a cylinder—a pointless project, in Miri's opinion—she laid down her pencil. "Are you thinking about Maudie?" she whispered.

Molly's eyes darted guiltily away. "No. Nope," she said. Then, "Can we round up the decimals?"

Meanwhile, Ollie worked on the porch, with Miri silently cheering him on. Once it was finished, the hole in time would be plugged—she felt certain of it. Five little boards over the back door were no protection from the past, Miri knew. 1918 was waiting, just over that feeble hurdle, and if Miri realized it, she knew that Molly did, too. She could almost see the past, crouched outside the door like a wild animal, ready to eat Molly up.

You're not sure how it works, she reminded herself. But she was almost sure. Just as she had explained to Molly before, she felt certain that their house was a place where the barriers separating past and present were very, very thin. All the events, the lives, the pasts that had ever taken place inside the house were alive within its walls, still occurring, still existing, still being. The time that she and Molly lived in, the present, was only the container, the outermost shell holding in a million pasts. What was familiar to them—their bedroom, their living room, their kitchen—was the current version, and it formed sort of a lid over past versions, the way a bread's crust covered its interior. But the crust of the present could crack, and when it did, the past was ready to bubble up and fill the hole.

And that, Miri reasoned, was exactly what had happened when her father and Ollie knocked down the back porch: the previous porch, existing all the while trapped under the lid of the one they'd demolished, floated to the surface of time, bringing with it the whole world of its own present—1918.

It made sense, in its own magic way, but there was still plenty to wonder about. If, for instance, her father had happened to step out of the empty doorframe, would he have landed in 1918? Or, since Miri was pretty sure that the porch hadn't existed *only* in 1918—would the magic have whisked him off to another year? And that question was minor compared with the mystery of the front door. Why did it bring them back to the twenty-first century? Miri spent a useless hour inspecting the door for clues before she'd had an inspiration.

"Ollie?" she called, leaning out a kitchen window. "I think the front door is rotting."

Ollie's thin face lit up. "I better take a look," he said, and hurried around the house to the front. A long ten minutes passed as he peered at the surface of the door. Finally, he turned to Miri. "No rot," he said bitterly. "Not a thing."

"But what about all those dark spots right there?"

"That? That's the *wood*." He shook his head at her ignorance. "It's just old."

Bingo! "How old?" asked Miri at once.

"Old."

"As old as the house?" she pressed.

Ollie stepped back and looked thoughtfully at the house. "Yep."

It wasn't exactly scientific proof, but it was good enough for Miri. The door had stayed the same, unchanged since the beginning of the house. Nothing had happened to it, so it had simply moved along with time into the present. All its pasts were locked under the crust of now, meaning that it would always open into the present. Miri was grateful for that, at least.

There were other questions, of course, questions about how, who, and why, but Miri didn't worry much about them. She was too busy worrying about Molly. When the new porch was built, the leak in time would be plugged, and 1918 would be unreachable. Molly would have no choice but to remain where she was—where she belonged. If staring could hammer nails into boards, the new porch would have been finished, but as it was, Miri had to be patient as Ollie measured, pounded, and hauled.

"Oooh, he's the ma-an!" Miri looked up from her thoughts. Ray was doing a victory dance. "Oooh," he yodeled, waggling the lettuce over his head, "Ray's the winner and you"—he pointed at Robbie—"are the big fat loser-boy, uh-huh!"

Since neither of her brothers had ever won a game without insulting the loser, Miri didn't understand why they both continued to be insulted by the insults. Why couldn't they just ignore them? But they never could. Robbie, flushed with rage, stopped, pivoted, and charged at Ray. "*Swarm!*" he bellowed over his shoulder.

Miri shook her head but dutifully began to run. Swarm was a Gill tradition, a sacred obligation, and no one was allowed to question it, much less ignore it. When a swarm was called, all available brothers and sisters were required to descend on the enemy like flies, head-butting, lunging, poking, dodging back and forth, side to side, up and down, until the victim surrendered in confusion. The point was not to hurt the target, but to harness the power of the mob for the greater Gill good. Swarming parents had long been forbidden, but swarming classmates, babysitters, and misbehaving siblings was very effective. Robbie, Miri, Molly, and the two little girls zoomed toward Ray, buzzing monotonously like overgrown mosquitoes.

"Get outta here!" he cried, swatting at the closing circle of siblings. "Haters! I caught it! I won! Cut it out!"

Suddenly, they heard the tingling sound of breaking glass.

All six children went still and silent, too used to being the manufacturers of such sounds to be certain that they hadn't caused it.

"Mama?" called Nora anxiously.

"Sorry!" It was Ollie's voice, coming from inside the house. "Aah, sorry about that. Sorry, Pammy!"

After a minute or two, their mother appeared on the front porch, looking harassed. "Don't worry, kids. Ollie just broke one of the windows in the living room. Don't worry about it." Her eyes fell on the bedraggled lettuce under Ray's arm. "That's enough lettuce-ball anyway, kids. Come on in. You shouldn't play with your food."

Reluctantly, they straggled in, Miri last of all.

Ahead of her, Ray paused at the doorway to the living room. "Whoa, Ollie!" he yelped. "You *killed* that window, man!"

Miri winced when she saw it. Ollie hadn't just broken the glass. He had torn out the entire window frame, leaving a ragged hole on one side of the room. The wooden window frame, with bits of shattered glass still attached, was propped mournfully in a corner.

"Rot," said Ollie briefly, sweeping up glass with a little broom. "Look at that wood."

"You had to tear out the whole thing?" Miri asked. Poor house.

Ollie nodded briskly. "Gotta do it while the weather's still okay. I'm gonna tarp up the hole, of course. Just be a couple of days."

Their mother hurried into the room. "Frank says don't start anything else without showing him first. Okay?"

Ollie looked offended. "It was rotten." He pointed to the remains of the window. "And so's the bathroom window upstairs. The whole frame, you could stick your finger through it—"

"No," said Mom firmly. "No new projects without showing Frank first. Okay?" She waited, her eyebrows raised.

Ollie heaved the sigh of the misunderstood. "If you say so."

· · ·

"Friday!" shouted Miri the next morning when her alarm went off. "Friday. Get up!" The shouting was for Molly, who never heard alarms. "Get up! *Up!*"

No movement below.

Miri hauled herself to the edge of the top bunk and looked down. Molly was awake. She lay flat in her bed with her hands folded on her chest like a corpse. "I feel terrible," she said in a whisper.

"Terrible?" Miri put on her glasses and inspected her sister. Was she lying? She did look weird, but maybe it was just how her hands were folded. "Which part of you?" she asked suspiciously.

"I'm hot," said Molly. "And my head hurts."

"Huh," said Miri. "You want me to get Mom?"

Molly nodded.

There followed Mom's sick-kid bustle. Thermometer! Juice! Aspirin! All other children warned to stay away!

"No one else is allowed to get sick," announced Mom, placing five bowls of applesauce on the kitchen table. "That goes for you, too," she said to Cookie, who had settled herself in the middle of the floor so that everyone had to step over her.

"Me and Robbie can't get sick," said Ray, gulping milk. "We have to do that thing tomorrow."

"Robbie and I," said Mom.

"What thing?" asked Dad, plopping an enormous stack of toast on the table.

"That war thing," said Ray, jamming an entire piece of toast in his mouth.

"What?" asked Mom.

Ray swallowed and said it again.

"That depends," said Mom, "on whether Robbie's English paper is done by tomorrow."

"Stalky!" protested Robbie.

"Excuse me?"

"He's trying to make it a word," explained Ray. "It means really lame and annoying."

This was followed by a lecture about rudeness that Miri didn't listen to. "Does she have a fever?" she asked suddenly.

"What? Oh, Molly. Yup, a little one," her mother said. "No big deal, but she shouldn't go to school."

"I'm sick, too," said Nora. She pressed her hand against her stomach.

"Oh, that's terrible!" said Dad. "I'd better eat that toast for you." He reached toward her plate.

Nora grabbed her toast, which was glinting with cinnamon sugar. "I'm not all the way sick," she said.

• • •

At the bus stop, Miri watched the white puffs of her breath melt into the bright, sharp sky. It was almost cold. The elementary-school bus came, and Nell and Nora clambered on, a trace of regret for her lost sickness crossing Nora's face as she went.

Now the middle-school bus appeared over the crest of the road. As her brothers put down the branches they'd been poking each other with and shrugged their backpacks on, Miri realized what she was going to do.

"Guys!" she said quickly. "I'm not going to school

today." She hitched her backpack up. "Don't tell, okay?"

They stared at her in disbelief. "Wait—what?" Robbie said. "You're cutting?"

"How come?" demanded Ray.

"You getting on this bus or what?" called the bus driver, the grumpy one who liked only Molly.

"There's something I have to do," Miri said to her brothers in an undertone. To the bus driver, she called, "I feel sick. I feel like I might throw up."

"Stay off my bus, girl," said the driver.

Ray whistled admiringly. "Way to lie, Miri!" he whispered.

Robbie's blue eyes narrowed. "You know you're going to get busted, right?" She nodded. He shook his head and followed Ray onto the bus.

A few minutes later, Miri was racing from bush to bush, ever closer to the house. It was too bad the rhododendrons weren't there anymore, she reflected as she ran. They made great cover. Still, it wasn't too hard to find a hiding place. She hunkered down among the blackberry windmills that grew where the barn had been in 1918. It was sort of stickery and sort of damp, but she could see everyone who entered or left the house.

The first one out was her father, running down the front stairs with an armful of papers. Whoops, running back up the front stairs. And now out again, slamming himself into his car, chugging away down the driveway.

Then there was a long gap, almost an hour. Miri was forced to turn to her social studies textbook for amusement: "Mesopotamia: Land Between Rivers, Land Between Time." What does that even mean? she thought.

"Okay, honey, I'm leaving!" Miri's mother called as she swirled out of the house. "Feel better! Drink water! Call Daddy if you need anything!" She was wearing what she called her professor costume, and she looked pretty and busy, dashing for her car with her briefcase swinging.

Miri waited a bit longer. And then a little longer, for good measure. When she finally rose, her legs felt like Styrofoam. She let herself in the front door without making a sound. The hall was still, except for the golden dust floating gently in the sunlight and the ticking of the clock. Miri glided toward the kitchen like a ghost.

It was exactly what she'd expected to see, but her stomach sank anyway: Molly stood at the open back door, an enormous hammer in her hand, studying the boards that barred her way. As Miri watched, Molly sighed and hoisted up the hammer for her first stroke.

"Going someplace?"

Molly whirled around, her eyes wide with panic, the hammer dropping like a stone to her side. "What?" she stammered. "What are you doing here?"

Her shock steadied Miri. "Same thing you're doing," she said coldly. "Lying." She crossed her arms over her chest.

Molly looked at the floor. The hammer jiggled halfheartedly in the direction of the door. "I'm taking the boards down," she muttered.

"Why?" snapped Miri.

"You know."

"No, I don't."

Molly lifted her eyes, gray and pleading, to her sister. "I have to go back, Mir. I can save her. Maudie, I mean."

"I *know* who you mean," said Miri angrily. "How?"

Molly's gaze returned to the floor. "I can keep her from meeting my dad," she said softly.

"Got it," said Miri with a curt nod. "You keep Maudie from meeting your father, they don't get married, you don't get born, and she doesn't die. Is that the plan?"

"Yeah," mumbled Molly.

"Great plan," said Miri. She glared at Molly. "You don't get born. That's just great."

"No one will know," said Molly miserably. "Think about what happened when I came here. We erased the other past. No one remembers when I wasn't here."

"Except for us!" Miri was yelling now. "You and me—we remember! So it's fine with you if I have to be lonely and miss you, right? Think of what your grandma said—she said when you came here, that you were setting things *right*. And now you want to go back and mess everything up! You think I won't know you're gone?" She stamped her foot. "I will!"

Molly's gray eyes filled with tears. "Maybe not. Maybe I'll be erased from your memory. I hope."

"You *hope*? Don't you care? About me and Mom and Dad and the kids?" Miri couldn't stop shouting. "Why, all of a sudden, do you care more about

Maudie than about us? Is it like she's your real mom and our mom's just fake?"

There was a shocked silence. "Is that what you think I'm thinking?" asked Molly incredulously. She shook her head. "No. Maudie seems like—a really nice girl, that's all. I mean, sure, she's going to be my mother, but I don't even know her. She's not my mom; Mom's my mom." Molly frowned. "You don't think I *want* to do this, do you? I don't *want* to. I have to."

"That's ridiculous. You don't *have* to."

"Yes, I do." Molly sighed. "We've said it a million times. If the magic happens again, it'll mean that we're supposed to do something. It won't just be for fun; it won't be playing around. There's something we're supposed to do." She looked toward Miri. "Come on—haven't we always said that?" Miri nodded uneasily. They had said it, and Grandma May had confirmed it—magic was given for a reason. Magic didn't waste itself sending people through time for nothing. "So," Molly pressed, "what does it want me to do? Why did it send us back to 1918? Why did it let us meet Maudie?"

"I don't know," Miri admitted. "But," she added

quickly, "it doesn't mean you're supposed to keep yourself from being born." It couldn't mean that, she argued inside herself. It wouldn't.

"What else can it mean?" demanded Molly. "We met Maudie. And she was great, right? She doesn't deserve to die, and she sure doesn't deserve to die because of me. Right?"

"No!" said Miri. "Or yes! I don't know!"

Molly went on as though she hadn't spoken. "All this time, I wondered why I could remember both lives. It seemed wrong; it seemed like it meant I was detachable, like I had to keep remembering 1935 so I could go back to it. That's what I was scared of, and I was right."

"You don't have to go."

"Yeah, I do." Molly smiled bitterly. "I have to be returned, like clothes that don't fit. I know what's going to happen, and I *can* stop it, so I have to go back and stop it. Don't I?"

"No, you don't. That's not what it means, it can't be. . . ." Miri struggled to find another explanation, another argument, another anything.

Molly went on, almost talking to herself now. "I'm the only one who could do it. Nobody else could make the choice for me. Why else would I have been sent to see Maudie?" she asked again, her forehead furrowed. "There's only one reason I can think of. I'm supposed to keep her alive. And I can do that. So I should."

An idea flashed into Miri's mind. "Wait!"

Molly looked up, hopeful. "What?"

"It's too late! They've already met! They must've! I mean, they almost had to! He was inside and she was in the yard, but that's, what? Thirty feet apart? They must've met! So it's too late, nothing you can do—"

The glint of hope disappeared. "They didn't meet," said Molly.

"You don't know that—"

"Yes, I do," Molly said. "Because I know what she was wearing the first time he saw her, and it wasn't a nightgown. She was wearing a yellow dress. It was almost sunset, and he thought she was light, shining through the clouds."

"Wow." In spite of herself, Miri was impressed. "He told you that?"

"Yeah. Lots of times."

"Romantic."

"I guess." Molly's eyes dropped to the floor. After a moment's silence, she said, "I think I've figured out a way. You know, to keep them apart."

The resignation in her voice made Miri's heart hurt. "This isn't what you're supposed to do," she whispered. "It can't be." She swallowed, hard. "Please don't leave."

Molly cleared her throat and turned back to the door. "I tried to find the stairs from the yard a few days ago. I must've looked like a loon, trying to climb invisible stairs, but no one saw. Anyway, I couldn't do it, so I figured I have to go from inside the house. We know that works, right?"

"Why didn't you do it before now?" asked Miri. If she could just keep her talking . . .

"Ollie the Rot King," said Molly. "That guy's always around. But he told Mom he had to take the weekend off because of the reenactment. That's why I said I was sick." Abruptly, she lifted the hammer and slammed it against the top board. With a chalky squeal, the nail came loose.

Miri watched as the wall fell, board by board, until, with a final dry squawk, the last piece toppled away from the doorframe to the ground below.

Molly placed the hammer carefully on a nearby counter and turned to Miri. For a moment, they looked at each other in silence.

"Don't go!" begged Miri. "We're supposed to be sisters."

"I know. But we got *magic*," Molly said softly. "We have to deserve it." She turned to step over the threshold.

Miri's hand shot out to hold her back. But it was too late.

∾ CHAPTER ∾

7

"ARE YOU ALL RIGHT?" called Miri, peering over the rim of the doorway. Inside her ribs, her heart was galloping.

"Yeah," said Molly uncertainly from the dirt below. When the new porch was built, it would be the dirt under the porch. Right now, it was the dirt you fell in if you stepped out the back door thinking that you were going to be held up by an invisible floor. "It didn't work, did it?" she asked, a little dazed.

Miri shook her head and jumped down beside Molly, trying to mask her roaring happiness. *Not gone! Still here!*

"Why not, though?" Molly stretched out her hand.

Miri pulled her sister to her feet. *Still here! With*

me! Together, they scanned the construction zone. Twenty thick posts marked out a perimeter, an outline of the porch to come. It was only a suggestion of the future, but it was, apparently, enough to obliterate the past. "See that?" said Miri, waving at the posts. "I think that's enough to lock out the past."

"But it's not finished. It's not a porch. It's just a border."

Miri nodded. "I know, but I think that's all it takes. The past is covered up by the present." She explained her ideas about the house and time to Molly.

"That's pretty much the same thing I came up with." Molly nodded. She lifted her eyes to Miri's. "Am I safe?" she whispered. "Is the hole in time closed?"

"Closed," Miri said, trying to suppress a smile. "Locked. You can't go back."

"I can't go back," Molly repeated obediently.

Miri shook her head. She couldn't help grinning.

"So it's probably okay that I got born," Molly continued, her eyes fixed on Miri's.

"Right," Miri said. "It's out of your control. So the magic must want you to stay here, with us." *Saved!*

Molly's face smoothed with relief, and she let out a long breath. "I've been freaking out all week," she confided.

"I know. I could tell."

"I didn't want to, you know," Molly said, watching Miri.

Miri nodded. "I know. It's okay." *Here forever!*

Molly's smile was like light breaking through clouds. She gave a little bounce on her toes and stretched out her arms, just to feel the air. "Boy, am I starving! I couldn't eat anything this morning— too busy freaking out. Let's go *eat*. Let's have toast and cereal and eggs!"

Miri reached out and flapped her sister's braid. "Race you!"

The two girls swerved around Ollie's stack of pink boards and hurtled along the side of the house to the front stairs, laughing about nothing as they went.

"I win!" called Miri, bounding in the door.

"Only because I'm weak from not eating," said Molly, banging the door behind her. "We could make cheese omelets—"

Suddenly, she broke off.

Miri, halfway down the hall, stopped. "Molly?"

Molly stood, frozen, in the doorway of the living room.

"What?"

Molly turned, and when Miri saw her face, her stomach flopped. *"What?"*

"The hole in time. It's not closed," said Molly. "It's just in a different place." She pointed at the tarp-covered space where the window had been and took a shaky breath. "I guess I have to"—she licked her lips—"you know."

Miri nodded. Magic had defeated them. "We'll do it together." She drew up next to her sister, facing the hateful plastic that covered the hateful emptiness that held the hateful past.

"You'd go with me?" Molly's voice rose. "Really?"

"We're a team, right?" answered Miri. She couldn't change what the magic seemed to want. She couldn't argue with it. The only thing she could do was stay with Molly until the last possible moment— but she didn't want to think about the last possible moment. "We're a team." She grabbed a handful of tarp and pushed it aside.

Together, the girls settled themselves on the rough edge of the wall and looked out at the side yard, at the straggly flowers and that wide expanse of grass ending in the faraway blackberry tangle. Molly glanced down to the ground beneath the window, where rhododendron bushes would be when they landed. "This is going to hurt," she said gloomily.

Miri nodded. It was. "Maybe the magic will throw us over the bushes. Just to be nice."

Molly made a face. "Don't count on it."

"Ready?" said Miri.

"Set," they said together.

"Go." They jumped.

. . .

They stood, brushing the dirt from their hands.

"I wonder what happened to the rhododendrons," said Molly, looking around. "They were here last week."

Miri didn't answer. The bushes had disappeared, replaced by stubbly grass that ran from the barn in the distance right up to the side of the house. She shifted nervously, pressing herself against the wood behind her. Though there was no one in sight, she had a strong urge to hide.

"Okay," said Molly. "The first thing we have to do is find him. Pat Gardner."

"Find him," echoed Miri, glancing around. Something was strange. Off.

"He's in Paxton," Molly said. "He's staying with his friend Sam. I guess we'll just look around until we see him. Paxton's pretty small and . . ." She trailed off, watching Miri's eyes dart back and forth. "What?"

Miri shook her head. She didn't know. "Something's weird. I can't put my finger on it, but—it's awful quiet."

It was awful quiet. Not a sound in the whole world around them, only a waiting silence. No birds, no animal sounds at all. Miri looked toward the barn—why weren't the chickens making a racket? Chickens always made a racket. And what about the pigs? There should at least be a snort or two from the pigs. Even the sky was empty, a flat gray expanse like dull metal. She shivered a little and flattened herself even more against the house.

But Molly was focusing with grim determination on the task in front of her, not the eerie silence. "When we find him, I'm going to say Flo has the influenza. It was a big deal in 1918, the flu. I looked it up. He for sure won't come to the house if she's got it."

Miri nodded and took a step away from the house. The sense of something wrong was almost overpowering. She edged closer to her sister and scanned the scene again. "Mols?"

"Hm?"

"Nothing."

They moved slowly toward the front yard. Miri looked down the sloping yard toward the road. The hedge that marked the bottom of the yard in the twenty-first century had not yet been dreamed of, and the white fence that stood in its place ran only a little ways and then broke off abruptly in a shattered heap of boards. Beyond it, Miri could see a bare dirt road curving away into a dry, gray distance.

"Wait." Miri stopped short, her eyes darting over the wide downhill swath of grass. "Where's the tree?" The enormous elm tree was nowhere to be seen. Absurdly, she turned in a circle, as though it might have picked itself up and moved to another part of the yard in her absence.

And then she saw something that caused her to

forget the tree altogether: the house. It had shrunk. It was missing most of its second story, all of its turret, and half the front porch. The half-porch that remained came to a jagged end, its broken floor slanting precariously over the yard as if it had been chewed off, its railing dangling in empty space. The stained glass around the door was gone, and the door itself hung slightly open. Beside her, Molly was seeing the same thing. They turned to each other in disbelief. "This isn't—" Molly began, her eyes wide.

"1918," Miri finished.

They stared blankly at each other. "But when?" asked Molly in a whisper.

"But why?" asked Miri.

. . .

The stillness cracked like an egg.

A thundering blast exploded from the road, and suddenly the empty air was peppered with hollow cracks, louder and louder—so loud, so close, that Miri instinctively threw her hands over her face and dropped to her knees.

"*No!*" Molly shrieked, and Miri felt herself yanked upward. With a flying leap, Molly ran, pulling Miri behind her as the air filled with smoke, and fire blazed in thin, knifelike streaks through the thick white clouds.

"What, what, what," Miri chattered, her legs stumbling forward, collapsing, wobbling up again. She couldn't, she couldn't—she was made of jelly, her legs wouldn't hold her, and she fell again, dragging Molly down with her. "Wha, wha, wha—" she babbled, before she was interrupted by an unearthly screech like a hundred beasts—

"Shh!" Molly pushed her flat in the weeds and flung herself alongside. "Head down," she whispered in Miri's ear, and Miri obeyed, burrowing gladly into the solid dirt. Flat as she was, she was also at the top of the sloping yard, and between the dry brown stalks, she could see everything that was happening on the road. She saw shapes appear in the smoke; she saw them fumble forward, smash together, drop apart, disappear. She saw a man topple backward from his saddle, his mouth open in a cry lost in the noise; she saw a horse, massive and black, reel sideways. Then she looked upward, and there, above the mayhem, the empty circle of sky whirled.

"Close your eyes," whispered Molly as something

whined through the air over their heads and chunked into the side of the barn nearby.

Miri tried but she couldn't remember how. She couldn't even blink. She could only stare wide-eyed as fire flickered through white smoke and thunderous cracks filled the air. "Wha, wha, wha—" she gasped, and Molly's hand, clammy but reassuringly alive, came around and covered her mouth.

"It's okay," she whispered. "I know what it is. We'll be okay."

Miri grunted in helpless fear until the hand closed more tightly over her mouth.

Again and again, the whining spirals came over their heads and thudded into the barn. Hoofbeats made the earth shudder. Yowls and shrieks rose through the smoke. And then, above it all, there was a long, high squeal. Through the haze, Miri watched a horse rising, rising, rising, until it was nearly vertical, and the boy astride it slid to the ground and disappeared.

The horse flopped sideways, hooves up and then down.

Suddenly, as though a switch had been flipped, the thundering cracks stopped and voices rose from all around: shouting and cries, dozens of them, all at once: *"Re*mount!" "Stand down!" "Sir?" "Stand down, I say!" "Sir—" "Full retreat—" "Upperville—" "No, sir—"

A huge man loomed out of the smoke, gun in hand. Bizarrely, he was laughing, laughing hard as though he'd heard the funniest joke in the world. As Miri watched, he turned and fired his gun carelessly into the throng of men and smoke behind him.

"Hold fire!" someone screamed, and the man laughed harder and shot again.

"Run!"

There was a tiny, frozen second of silence, and then a ringing clatter, an earth-shaking thunder of hooves, and a wall of dust rose from the road.

Miri felt Molly go limp against her back. "It's over."

Miri panted like a dog. Her mouth wouldn't make words.

"Don't move," Molly breathed.

Miri blinked in answer. She couldn't have moved if she wanted to. Before her, a ghost on horseback rose out of the weeds. No, not a ghost. It was a man, a man in a gray coat covered with white dust. He wheeled his equally dusty horse around, and she saw that he was grinning. "Hern!" he whooped.

"Yessir!" A short man with a drooping mustache and a dirty gray uniform scrambled into view.

"Hern and Carter! Tie up the horses and tend to those who're still alive. We're gonna trail the others!"

A big man, the same one who had fired so casually into the crowd, appeared alongside the ghostly horse and rider. He was still laughing. "Colonel! Let me come along and give 'em some hell. I'll pick 'em clean!"

The Colonel pulled up on his horse and glared down at him. "You'll follow orders, Carter. And you, Hern. We'll come back for you." He glanced over his shoulder at the men scattered over the road. "I want those Yankees tended to, you hear? I don't want 'em dead." He turned to give Carter a piercing look. "You hear me, Carter?"

"You're just going to hang 'em anyway," said Carter sulkily.

"Maybe so," said the Colonel. "But they've got to be alive. I want Yankee prisoners, not Yankee corpses. That clear? Carter?"

"I'm a soldier, not a doctor," Carter sniffed.

Miri saw the Colonel's face. So did Carter. "Yessir," he mumbled.

The Colonel started to move off and then had second thoughts. "Don't try to tell me they died, either, Carter. I'll have you shot." And with that, he was off, tearing down the road in a plume of dust.

For a minute, Hern and Carter looked after the galloping figure. The one named Carter spat into the grass. "I believe we just got skunked, Hern."

"You got skunked," said Hern in a sour voice.

Molly's hand closed around Miri's arm. "Soon as they turn around, we run into the barn," she breathed.

Miri nodded, the functional part of her brain thankful that Molly was taking charge. She herself was stiff with fear; her mind was dashing about like a hunted rabbit. What was going on? Who were these guys? Soldiers? What for? And what would they do if they saw her?

The last question was probably the most important. Miri turned her head a fraction of an inch and saw that the two men were still looking after the retreating Colonel. "Pah!" Carter said bitterly. "Do I look like a stable boy? Do I look like a nursemaid?"

Hern sighed and tucked his pistol into his belt. "Guess the Colonel thinks so."

From Miri's vantage point, Carter just looked scary. He was enormous, and he was furious, and the combination looked deadly. His face was boiling with anger, his eyes were weirdly pale, and two of his fingers were jerking convulsively. For a moment, he stood stiff and rigid, then suddenly, he bent down, seized a rock, and hurled it with all his might at the barn. Miri heard the wood crack. She wished there were something more solid than grass between them.

"Now, Carter," said Hern uneasily. "Colonel said we was to pick up the wounded."

Carter ignored him. "Colonel's got no right to leave me behind," he said through his teeth. "I'm the best Ranger he's got, and he knows it. If he gets anything, it's because of me, and I deserve my share of the pickings. That Yankee captain had a gold watch, I'd bet my life on it, and I should get it. I shot more of them than anyone. I shot that fool lieutenant over there, and I got both the men in the ditch, too." He tallied them up like the score of a game. "And look! That boy's about done for. That's four!"

"Let's go tie up them horses," suggested Hern.

What about the wounded men? thought Miri. In spite of Molly's arm, she lifted her head a bit, just enough to see. Immediately, she wished she hadn't. A soldier lay in the road, his blue jacket pocked with holes, his eyes fixed on the empty sky. She looked away and saw the boy who'd been thrown off his horse; he had fallen on his back, and to Miri's surprise, he was still alive. He was trying to push himself through the weeds with the heel of his boot: a weak shove, a pause while he gulped for air, another shove. His blue coat was stained dark, with blood or sweat, Miri couldn't tell.

A horse whinnied nervously as Hern approached on one side, Carter on the other, stepping over the soldier in the road as if he didn't see him.

"Now," breathed Molly. Clutching Miri's hand, she rose in one quick movement, and they ran, crouching, toward the barn. They zigzagged around its weathered corner and lunged for the door. There—they made it. Inside the barn, they collapsed on a meager pile of hay against a wall.

"What—what the *heck* is going on?" demanded Miri in a whisper-shout.

"I'm pretty sure," Molly said, low, "that we're in the middle of the war."

"*What* war? There's no *war* in our front yard!"

"There was," Molly said. "The big one. The Civil War."

"The Civil War? But that's—that's *crazy*," Miri blurted. "That was a million years ago!"

Molly blinked at her. "No, it wasn't."

"But—but—" sputtered Miri, "it can't be. It's ridiculous." The Civil War? Impossible! The Civil War was something unimaginably ancient, something that didn't actually exist in the same three-dimensional world she did. As she continued to stutter her objections, she saw, again, the smoke and fire, heard the chunking of metal into wood, the heavy breathing of horses and men, all of them crackling with movement and energy. It couldn't be the Civil War. The Civil War was black-and-white pictures, educational videos, and long books with footnotes. "They don't look like history," she said weakly. "They look like regular people."

"It was the 1860s, not the Jurassic period," began Molly, but before she could say more, there was a heavy thud against the outer wall of the barn.

"Why, my gracious, I must've dropped him," snickered Carter.

"Help me," choked a voice.

Miri and Molly looked at each other, horrified, and they heard Hern mutter, "Colonel said not to kill 'em."

"Do you see me killing anyone?" asked Carter.

"Bandage?" croaked the man. "Could I get a bandage—"

"Bandage?" asked Carter. "I wouldn't waste an inch of cloth on a Yankee dog like you. Use that piece of trash you call a shirt if you want a bandage." There was a shifting sound as the man struggled with his shirt, and then Carter said, "Look at that fool boy, pushing himself through the dirt. Does he think we're blind?"

"Is that Jamie?" The wounded man's voice lifted with hope. "He's still—he's not—he's alive?"

"I'm ashamed to say that he is," Carter said bitterly. "Don't know how I missed such an easy shot."

Again, Miri saw him, laughing as he fired his gun into the crowd. A lump of anger rose in her throat. Molly squeezed her hand and made a gesture that meant *Hush*.

"I guess we gotta haul him up here," said Hern regretfully.

"Wait," said Carter. "Wait a few minutes, and he'll die. I wager he'll die before he gets to the road. I'll put five dollars on it."

"You don't got five dollars," said Hern. "Colonel said to keep 'em alive. Come on." Footsteps kicked through grass and died away.

Carter heaved a dramatic sigh and followed.

Miri turned to Molly. Who are these guys? she mouthed.

"Southerners," breathed Molly. "Rebels. Confederates. Anyone in a gray coat is fighting for the South. Blue coats are the Yankees." She gave Miri a look. "The Yankees are the Northerners."

"I know *that*," said Miri defensively. She pictured the men lying in the road. They were wearing blue. "I thought the Yankees won."

"Yeah, in the end, but not the whole time. And this wasn't a big battle. This was just a few soldiers."

It had seemed big enough to Miri. "The guy on the other side of the wall, he's their prisoner?" she whispered, and Molly nodded. What a rotten deal. First you had to fight and maybe die, and then, if you lost, you were taken prisoner by your enemies.

Molly put her finger to her lips as Carter returned. "I am not cut out for heavy lifting," he drawled, and the wall of the barn shook as another body crashed into it. It wasn't the boy, was it? thought Miri incredulously. They wouldn't throw a boy so badly wounded on the ground like that, would they? He'd never survive it. She heard a tiny whimper and dug her fingernails into her palm in agonized sympathy.

"Jamie?" asked his friend gently. "Jamie?"

"Isn't that sweet?" Carter cooed, and Miri sent waves of loathing through the barn wall.

"He don't look so good," observed Hern.

"Sit up, now, boy! Come on, lad!" urged the wounded soldier. His voice was stronger than it had been—Miri guessed that the shirt-bandage had helped. But Jamie was silent. "Help me get him up," pleaded the man. "He's hardly breathing, pitched over like he is."

"Don't touch him, Hern!" snapped Carter. "What're you thinking? He's the enemy!"

"Colonel said not to kill 'em," Hern said doggedly. Stupid but stubborn, Miri thought. Not as bad as Carter.

"Come now," pleaded the wounded man. "Please!

Just lift him a little, and I can do the rest. Come on, Jamie, old boy."

"Colonel said not to kill them," repeated Hern.

"Oh, for the love of God, I am plagued by fools!" Carter bellowed. "All right, Hern, watch me: I will doctor the lad." He made a noise that Miri guessed was a laugh, but it sounded like a dog squealing, and she felt the flesh on the back of her neck shrivel a little. "It is my medical opinion that the boy has fainted. He needs to be brought around. Observe: the direct method." There was a sharp slap and a cry. Miri covered her mouth with her hands. Beside her, Molly sat rigidly, her eyes tightly shut.

"Why, look at that!" Carter giggled. "Look at him twitch. I should have been a doctor." Another slap.

"Stop!" yelled the wounded man. "You're going to kill him!"

"Stop that, Carter!" blustered Hern. "Colonel's going to shoot us if they're dead."

"No, no, he's getting better each time!" Carter snickered. "Watch!"

"Five hundred dollars in gold!" bellowed the soldier.

A sudden silence.

"Beg pardon?" asked Carter.

"Let us go," the soldier gasped. "Give me a horse. I'll pay five hundred dollars in gold."

"You don't have five hundred dollars in gold," said Carter. But Miri thought he sounded a little cautious.

"I do."

"Where?" demanded Carter. "Back home in your mattress?"

"No. Someplace near. I'll tell you if you let us go."

There was a pause. "How'd you get it?"

"We're guard detail," the man said. "All of us. Guard detail, trying to go north and get this gold onto the train east before you Rebs can blow up the tracks again."

Miri looked a question at Molly: What's guard detail?

The guys who guard the trains, Molly mouthed. I think.

Carter interrupted. "Where's the gold?" His elegant language got a lot simpler when he talked about money, Miri noticed.

"Carter," Hern whined. "We can't do this. Colonel needs prisoners. He said so."

"You can get yourself some other boys, easy," the soldier said quickly. "There's plenty of them right behind us. They sent down the rawest pack of babies I ever saw to watch over the railroad crew. They're coming out of Fisher's Hill, not six hours behind us. You just sit right here, you'll catch yourself more prisoners than you know what to do with. Your Colonel won't care, and you'll be five hundred dollars richer. And"—he shifted against the wall—"me and Jamie will be off your hands." His voice cracked, and Miri could hear the panic right below the surface. He was bargaining for his life, his life and Jamie's, and he'd reached the moment when the balance would tip in one direction or the other. Miri closed her eyes and added her hopes to the soldier's. Come on, she urged Hern and Carter. Say yes.

The silence stretched out. "Bird in the hand," Carter said.

"Five hundred dollars," Hern said thoughtfully.

"In gold," said Carter, luxuriating in the word. "You can't do better than gold."

Miri and the soldier exhaled with relief. Then he asked, "How do I know you won't shoot me in the back once you got the money?" A good question, in Miri's opinion.

But Carter was offended. "You dare to judge my honor by your own, you swine?" he boomed. "I am a Carter of Virginia and a gentleman. Were it not for my honor, I'd shoot you now and hunt out the money myself. I'd do it with pleasure."

The soldier sniffled. "It's pretty well hid. Not so easy to find."

There was a pause, and then Carter said, "I give you my word of honor, as a Carter, before Hern here as witness, that I won't shoot you in the back—or the head or any other place. I'll give you a horse, and I'll even help you get on it, once I have five hundred dollars in gold in my hand."

"What about me?" yelped Hern.

"Three hundred for me, two hundred for you," said Carter smoothly. "As I have conducted the negotiations."

There was a silence. "Two hundred," Hern sighed. "But don't you go cheating me." Miri and Molly exchanged glances. Hern was going to be cheated.

Carter stamped his boot. "Enough! Let's see this gold!"

The man cleared his throat. "Black horse lying over there. Hundred in the right saddlebag, inside a bandage. Another hundred down in the ditch, on the buckskin—there's a pocket in the saddle blanket. That white mare, that ugly one over there? She's got a hundred somewheres on her, dunno where. That fellow there, see him? Another hundred, I think in his boot. I got the other. Right here." There was a sound as he adjusted himself. "You can probably get it easier than I—have a care!" he squealed as he was searched roughly.

Miri heard grass swish as Carter and Hern strode away. Minutes passed with bridles rattling softly in the distance and pleased calls as the men found their treasure.

Against the barn, the soldier murmured encouragement to Jamie. "Steady, son. Almost there. Yep, that's it, that's it, he's got Turcott's hundred, whoops. There. Just breathe easy; it's almost done—" Miri wondered if Jamie heard any of it. Stay alive, she ordered him silently. "Now, see, that tall Reb's tossed up a bag of gold like it don't weigh a thing. Aw, the mare don't like him; she's going to kick him—hah!— he almost shot his own foot off. Wish he had. He's giving his pistol to the other one to hold, and, oh, now he's got her. You just keep breathing, Jamie. They got most all of it now, just the one more, and then we can—" He broke off as the men returned and called out eagerly, "Found it all? That's fine. Now, if you'll see to Jamie here, please. Just put him on the horse, and I'll get myself up—"

There was a snicker. "I don't recall saying anything about the boy," Carter said. "I said I'd give you a horse. I said I'd help you onto it. I didn't say a thing about a boy."

Miri and Molly looked at each other, hating Carter.

"No!" cried the soldier. "You made a bargain! Jamie, too! He's my own nephew, my sister's lad. I can't leave him behind!"

"Carter." It was Hern's voice. "We made a deal."

"I made a deal for one," said Carter airily. "Not two. Two will cost more."

"I ain't got any more!" shrilled the soldier. "You promised. On your honor, you said!"

"I did no such thing, Yankee, and I'll shoot anyone who says I did," Carter said in a tight voice. "This boy is a prisoner of war, and I'd need a good deal more gold to let him go."

"You scoundrel! You lying sinner!" The soldier

was almost sobbing with helpless fury. "You low-down, two-bit cheat!"

"Shut your mouth, Yankee," said Carter.

But the soldier was too furious to stop. "You lying dog, you dirt-licking—"

There was crunch of boot against rib, and a strangled yelp.

"Now, Carter!" begged Hern. "Stop that, Carter!"

"I'll not be insulted by a Yankee. Any man who calls me a liar pays the price," Carter snapped. Then, with a guffaw, "No! Better yet, the boy pays the price!"

⌁ CHAPTER ⌁

8

"No!"

Without even knowing what she was doing, Miri was on her feet. "No!" she cried, catapulting for the door. She couldn't bear it. He was going to do something awful to Jamie, and she couldn't bear it. "He didn't do anything!" she shrieked. "Leave him alone, leave him alone, *leave him alone*!" And then she was outside, in the bright, empty light, charging for Carter.

He spun around, startled, and she threw herself at him, kicking and slapping at whatever she could reach.

"Stop it! Stop it! Leave him alone!" she screeched as she pounded and pummeled, but even fueled by fury, her fists made no headway. It was like hitting a tree.

An angry tree. "What the devil's this?" Carter shouted, swatting at her. "Get off me, you catamount!" He twisted to avoid her, and she managed to land a punch to his chin. It was a weak blow, but she surprised him and he bit his tongue. "Ow!" he bellowed, diving at her.

Miri dodged away—eleven years with Ray and Robbie had taught her that much, at least—and stuck out her tongue. "Can't catch me, you freak!" she cried. Maybe if she made him mad enough, he would chase her, and the soldier and Jamie would have a chance to slip away. "Try it! Try to catch me!" she taunted. Sometimes big people were awkward and slow.

Not Carter. He let out an exasperated snort, and she felt his enormous hand close like steel around her arm. He lifted her up and shook her like a doll. "Stupid child! Quit dancing about!" He jerked Miri close to his face, and for a split second, they gazed at each other. His eyes were yellowish, like marbles, and as he looked at her, Miri saw a change come over his face; standard adult aggravation at a kid's interference transformed before her eyes into something much weirder, something it took her a second to identify: anticipation. His mouth spread into a smile. "Why," he murmured, "you look just like my little sister." He snickered. "But perhaps you'll have better luck."

Miri gave an involuntary shudder: There was nothing as scary as people who liked to be scary. Carter's pale eyes gleamed with satisfaction as she twisted in his grip, trying to think. Think, she urged herself. Think quick, like Molly. Right, okay, he'll probably break my arm in a second, so I need to hurt him as much as I can before that. She drew back her foot, slammed him in the knee, and saw his eyes open wide with surprise and pain.

She cringed, waiting for him to hit her, but to her astonishment, he went suddenly still. Maybe I really hurt him, she thought, encouraged. "Go! Go!" she shouted over her shoulder at the soldier against the barn, "Take Jamie and go!"

There was a pause. "That all right, missy?" the soldier asked politely.

"Yes," said Molly's voice. Miri wriggled in Carter's grip, trying to see around him. "Let go of her," Molly ordered, and Carter's hand opened.

Miri moved quickly out of his reach—and saw

the new balance of power. Molly stood behind Carter with a heavy iron pitchfork in her hands. Miri's eyes followed the long handle and came to rest on the five sharp metal points pressed into the back of Carter's neck. As Miri watched, Molly began to edge around him, the needle-sharp points etching a thin circle of red in his neck. His eyes followed Molly's movement, narrowing slightly when Miri's hands joined Molly's to hold the pitchfork steady.

"Can you get Jamie up on the horse by your-self?" Molly called to the soldier.

"Uh, I believe so," he said eagerly. "I think so. If I can just—" Miri couldn't see what he was doing, but she heard him breathe heavily with effort. He was trying to stand up. "Sure do appreciate it, missy, you helping out the Union cause like this," he muttered as he fumbled and gasped. "I'll send a letter to—to—General Augur and, and—to General Grant himself, yessir, I mean ma'am. Whew!" There was a pause. "I'm up!"

"Hern!" Carter said in an agonized croak. "Shoot them, for God's sake!"

Hern! Miri had forgotten about him. She glanced desperately over her shoulder—where was Hern?

Hern's voice came from behind her. "I ain't shooting no little girls," he said with finality, and Miri let out a relieved breath. She saw that Molly was doing the same. "Seems to me like we got our five hundred dollars and we shoulda left well enough alone."

"Fool," said Carter through his teeth. "I reckon he's got another five hundred on him somewhere."

"No, he don't. The way I see it," Hern said, "we bargained on five hundred and they paid five hundred, and I ain't shooting them nor any little girl just 'cause she got you treed." He gave a sudden hacking laugh. "And, Carter, I never seen a better joke on you. Treed by two little girls! They got you fair and square—and they ain't so high as your elbow, either of 'em!"

Frustrated, furious, Carter made a lightning grab for the pitchfork—and gasped as Molly jabbed it hard into his neck. "Not so fast, buster!" she snapped. "One move and I'll poke it right in your eyes."

Hern guffawed. "You tell him, sister! Funniest dang thing I ever seen! Old Nick Carter! Beaten by a pair of girls! Haw!"

Beneath Hern's honks of laughter, they heard the repetitious mutter of the wounded man as he attempted to lift Jamie into the saddle. "Come on, boy, come on, Jamie, you're all right—"

Hern was still laughing when he strolled over to the struggling soldier. "Aw, you gonna bust a gut doing that. Here." Easily, he took the man under the arms and lifted him into the saddle. A second later, he handed the boy up to his uncle, who wrapped his arms around the still, limp body, mumbling his meaningless words of comfort.

As the horse started toward the road, the soldier turned to nod to Miri and Molly. "Thank you, missies. You, too, Johnny," he said to Hern. "And you," he said to Carter, "the devil's got a fire waiting for you."

For some reason, this sent Hern into fresh gales of honking. "Old Nick Carter!" he gasped, wiping the tears streaming from his eyes.

Suddenly, Carter straightened, despite the sharp prongs, his eyes on the road. "Here's the Colonel!"

The Colonel? Miri glanced nervously over her shoulder—and the pitchfork was wrenched from her grasp.

"Gotcha!" bellowed Carter, flinging the pitchfork aside and lunging for Molly.

She eluded him by a hair, dancing away from his fingers as they closed, and Miri saw her first long leap. "*House!*" she cried as she ran past.

House? Right! House! Miri tore toward it, with Carter thundering at her heels. "I'll teach you," he roared. "I'll make you pay!"

Molly ran like a deer, bounding up the grassy slope. Miri, always slower, prayed to the gods of speed and pelted forward as best she could. It was just before her, not the house she knew, but all she needed was the door, the familiar door—

Just ahead of her, Molly was scrambling up the stairs, reaching a hand back to pull her forward—

Miri heard Carter's triumphant cry of "Mine!" and felt the brush of his fingertips against her back. The touch gave her a burst of terror, and she sprang upward to clasp Molly's hand. Together, they hurled themselves at the wooden door, flung it wide, and jumped.

There was one final fraction of a second for Miri to twist around and scream "Loser!" into Carter's face. And then they smashed through the sickening web of time.

❖ CHAPTER ❖

9

COOKIE STEPPED DAINTILY into the kitchen and froze, aghast at the sight of Miri and Molly lying like fallen plums in the middle of the floor. After a worried moment, the kitten padded to Miri's side and placed a soft paw on her face.

"Yaah!" Miri shot upward in fright.

Molly lifted her head. "What happened?" she croaked.

"Oh. It's just Cookie." Miri exhaled in relief and lay down once more, setting the kitten on her stomach. "Hi, sweetie-kitty." After a moment, an uncontrollable purr spilled from Cookie as she snuggled into Miri's hand.

Molly edged closer, and her hand joined Miri's

in stroking the kitten's soft fur. Eyes—both kitten and girl—closed. For a while, the only sound in the kitchen was purring.

"Whatsamatter with you guys?"

Miri opened an eye. Four incredibly dirty sneakers, covered with inky words and pictures, stood inches from her face. She looked up. "Hi."

Ray and Robbie exchanged frowns. "You're on the *floor*," said Ray. "You're sleeping on the *floor*."

"Brilliant observation," yawned Molly.

They'd landed in the front hallway on their hands and knees, sick and frightened. When they'd stopped shaking, they crawled to the kitchen and collapsed in a dazed heap. After the mayhem of war, the tense wait inside the barn, the fight with Carter, running for their lives, and breaking through time, the girls felt like the wooden floor was the most comfortable surface ever invented.

"That's lame," concluded Ray.

"Listen, Mir." Robbie dropped his backpack next to her head with a floor-shaking thump. "We got you an excused absence, okay?"

Miri blinked at him. "You did? How?"

Identical grins flickered across her brothers' faces. "Never mind."

"No, really," she insisted. "How? Are you going to get in trouble?"

They snickered and shook their heads. "There's this girl—" began Robbie.

"Robbie," warned Ray. "She'll kill us, bro."

Robbie hesitated and decided against it. "So anyway, Mom won't know you cut." He bent to unzip his backpack. "And I got your guys's homework, too. You got some in Lang Arts and"—he stirred the dark bowels of his backpack—"you both got math."

"Gosh, Robbie." Miri was touched. "You checked all our classes? That was really nice." Actually, since Robbie rarely managed to bring home all his own homework, it was beyond nice; it was amazing.

Ray snorted. "He didn't. Some dumb girl, Abby something, she gave it to him. She said she was your-guys' best friend."

Miri and Molly looked at each other doubtfully. Abby who?

"Oooh, *Robbie*," squealed Ray, "tell your sisters to *text* me! We were going to hang out together at *your* house this Saturday!"

Robbie turned a little red, but he shrugged. "Whatever. We're not going to be here anyway."

"Oooh, *Robbie*, you just *have* to be there, I'm going to *hate* you if you aren't," sang Ray. He made a long, smacking kissy sound.

Just as he had intended, the kissy sound pushed Robbie over the edge. "Shut up!" he cried, slapping the back of his brother's head.

Ray ducked. "Oooh, Robbie," he cackled, "you're so *cute* when you're mad! You look just like Justin Bieber, except ugly!"

"Least I don't look like a butt," grumped Robbie.

"You're identical!" giggled Molly. "You both look like butts!"

In answer, Ray blew out his cheeks and pushed them inward, a maneuver that made him look, in fact, like a butt.

They all began to laugh, and then they couldn't stop. Miri and Molly rolled on the floor, while Robbie snorted in a manly style until Ray did it again, and he dissolved into hoots.

Laughing, Miri glanced around the old kitchen and thanked the magic for bringing her home. Home, home, wonderful, beautiful home. I love everything, she thought. She loved Molly, she loved her brothers, she loved Cookie. She loved the floor, she loved the sink, she loved the refrigerator, she loved every chipped plate and dirty dish stacked on the counter. "I love everything," she sighed.

Ray gave a long, wet sniffle. "That's so beautiful I could cry."

Robbie grinned. "I feel all different inside now. Let's sing."

Miri smiled. They could make fun of her. She didn't mind. Safe and happy, she reached out and wrapped her hands around Ray's ankles. It was an old game, years old, but Ray remembered and started to walk backward, pulling her across the floor.

"God, we haven't done that in forever," said Robbie. Molly caught hold of his ankles, and he smiled down at her. "Ready?"

∿ CHAPTER ∿

10

CLEANED, BRUSHED, READY FOR BED, Miri drifted slowly down the hallway, smoothing her fingertips along the dark wood of the wall. For some reason, doing this helped her think. And at the moment, she needed to think about Maudie. Maudie and 1918. "What do we already know?" she murmured to herself. They knew that magic was a way of setting things right. They knew that it didn't waste itself unless there was a reason.

That afternoon's trip had had a reason, an obvious one. They had been sent through time to save Jamie, anyone could see that. Miri paused to imagine Jamie grown up, maybe president of the United States: "And let me say that I owe my greatest thanks to two unknown girls who saved my life one long-ago day . . ."

It was a satisfying image. Miri proceeded to the even more satisfying image of Carter explaining his lack of prisoners to the Colonel. She hoped the Colonel *would* shoot him. Now stop that, she told herself sternly, and concentrate: Why 1918? Why had they been sent there? If Molly was actually supposed to interrupt the meeting between Maudie and Pat Gardner, why had the magic barred her way back? Why had it sent them smack into the Civil War and Carter instead?

Because they were supposed to save Jamie. Fine. Good. But then, why send them to 1918 to meet Maudie in the first place?

Miri sighed. She couldn't figure it out.

Her brothers' bedroom door opened, flooding the hallway with light. Miri blinked. "Mir!" called Robbie in a harassed whisper.

"Yeah?"

"What's, like, the point of *Julius Caesar*?"

"Got me," she said. "I never read it."

Hoarse, despairing curses filled the hallway. Miri didn't take them personally. Her parents had laid down the law at the dinner table that night: If Robbie didn't finish his essay on *Julius Caesar* by tomorrow morning, there would be no reenactment for him.

"But, Dad!" Robbie had protested. "It's not due until Monday! I'm going to write it on Sunday!"

"Okay," said Dad, poking his salad in search of croutons, "that's your choice, but you won't be doing any extracurricular activities until you finish your curricular ones. In other words"—he found a crouton and waved it—"no reenacting unless the essay is done."

"We promised we'd be there!" Ray protested. "Mr. Emory will kill us if we don't show. He'll flunk us."

"That's terrible," said Dad calmly. "I guess there's only one solution: write the essay before eleven tomorrow morning."

One little fact Robbie had omitted from this conversation was that he had not yet finished—or begun—reading *Julius Caesar*.

Ray was perched on the edge of the bed, reading furiously. "Okay," he called, "it's set in Rome."

"Duh!" moaned Robbie.

"Why don't you look it up on the Internet?" suggested Miri.

"Dad turned it off!" he yelped. "Can you believe that?"

Dad was pretty smart, Miri thought. "I don't know why you want to fight in a war anyway," she said. "They're awful."

"Like you know anything," Ray said scornfully.

Miri leaned against the doorframe, thinking, again, about the mysterious purposes of magic. Had she and Molly, perhaps, performed some service in 1918 without knowing it? Was it possible, for instance, that their presence had kept some tragic event from happening? Each tiny thing that touched them was changed a little, she supposed. She allowed her imagination to run free, picturing her foot as it stepped on a loose tree root, pressing it a fraction of an inch farther into the ground, so that the tree leaned by some microscopic amount in a new direction. Then, later—years later—when a great storm ripped the tree from the ground, that same microscopic slant would ensure that it fell away from, not onto, the innocent bystander sheltering under its branches, thus saving a life destined for—what?—something noble. Hmm. Maybe. Vague, but better than nothing. "Molly?" She leaned out of her brothers' doorway and yodeled up toward her own. "I have an idea!"

· · ·

That night, she dreamed of Carter. He wasn't chasing her, he wasn't even touching her. He was simply walking toward her. She could see him, far away but getting closer, closer, closer. She strained and struggled, but she couldn't move, couldn't get free, and he was coming. "I have gold!" she cried suddenly, hoping to escape.

He shook his head, laughing. "Loser." And he kept coming.

A small hand shook Miri's shoulder. "Shh," Molly murmured. "It's okay. Carter's not here."

"Was I yelling?" Miri mumbled.

"More like groaning. Move over." Miri heaved herself to one side and Molly slid in beside her. "Don't worry," she whispered. "It's all over. Over and done. Over and done." She repeated the comforting words until Miri stopped shivering. "Over and . . ."

Side by side, they returned to sleep.

· · ·

"Jeez!" squawked Molly, lurching up. "What was that?"

Miri fumbled for her glasses. "A door slamming, I think."

"Jeez," repeated Molly, flopping down again.

But there was no help for it. They were awake and it was morning. Sunlight bobbled through the curtains.

They tiptoed past Ray and Robbie's room, which was ominously silent, and found Nell and Nora in the kitchen, consuming syrup.

Nora looked up. "Daddy said Robbie's paper wasn't good and he couldn't go to the actment, and then Ray said who said it had to be good and Robbie'd been up till the middle of the night, but Daddy said he couldn't just say all the people's names, he had to say something else, and then Robbie was really, really mad and he said it wasn't fair and then he said a bad word, and then Mom said that did it, and then Robbie slammed the door."

Nell summarized. "Everyone's mad."

Her sisters looked worried, so Miri said cheerfully, "I'm not mad!" and boinged one of Nell's curls.

"Me neither!" said Molly. "What's for breakfast around here?"

But she and Miri raised anxious eyebrows at each other. Unfairness made Robbie crazy. Ray got mad loudly and often, but Robbie was different. He was more patient than his brother, more even-tempered and easy-going. The only time Robbie lost it was when he decided something wasn't fair, but when he lost it, he lost it big. He was the only Gill child ever to have been suspended, and that was for clobbering an eighth grader who wouldn't let a new kid sit down in the school lunchroom.

Miri and Molly tried to radiate jolly confidence as they made toast and poured juice. "So," said Molly, settling beside Nell with a plateful of jammy toast, "what are you guys doing today?"

Nell and Nora looked at each other and smiled. "Helping Fritz."

Fritz was in charge of trimming the Gill trees and mowing their enormous circle of lawn. He was tall, red-haired, and so shy he could barely speak. Nell and Nora loved him. On the days he came to work at their house, the two little girls followed him from one spot to another, talking, both at once, the whole time. "Maybe he doesn't mind," their mother said worriedly. "Maybe it's good for his social skills."

So, despite its thunderous beginning, the morning proceeded quietly. Fritz's lawn mower hummed, and occasionally the buzz of a drill was heard in the backyard, where Dad was attempting to make progress on the porch without Ollie.

"Where's Mom?" called Molly out the window.

Dad looked up, shading his eyes. "Grocery store."

Oh.

Miri sat down in front of her math homework, feeling flat. Yesterday had been awful, the scariest of her life; it had made her wish with all her heart that she would never experience magic again; it had made her love her simple, quiet, normal life.

And here it was. Her life. Simple. Quiet. Normal.

Restlessly, she got to her feet.

Molly looked up. "Where are you going?"

"I don't know," said Miri. "I feel—I don't know—not bored, exactly, but—something."

Molly nodded. "Let down?"

"Yeah! That's it! Let down!"

"Me too," said Molly. She kicked the table leg gently. "We don't know the end of the story. It feels unfinished."

That was it: unfinished. Miri wanted to know what happened to Jamie, to his uncle, to Carter, even to the Colonel. It seemed wrong that they had been thrust into that scene, made to act in it, and then sent home before it was over.

Miri plopped down again with a sigh. "Maybe we'll find out what happened someday."

"You don't think it's trying to make us study history, do you?" asked Molly.

Miri shook her fist at the kitchen wall. "This had better not be educational!" she cried.

They returned to their math. For a long time, the quiet was broken only by whispered numbers.

Miri glanced up. Nothing.

Okay. Negative seventy-five divided by point-seven-five. She stared at it blankly.

A rustle.

She glanced up.

A suppressed laugh.

Miri and Molly looked at each other and grinned. The boys. They were up to something. Probably something bad. Probably something that they'd enjoy now and regret later. Probably something Miri and Molly would want to see. Together, the two girls rose from their chairs.

Soft footsteps on the stairs.

A clinking rattle. "Shh," very soft.

Miri and Molly tiptoed into the hall. "What're you guys doing?" Molly said, and they turned—

Two soldiers in dark blue coats and crumpled caps stared at them. Miri felt the blood drain from her face. They've broken through, she thought, backing away. There's nothing between us and the war.

Then she saw: It was Ray and Robbie, dressed for their reenactment.

"Oh my gosh," she gasped.

Robbie looked at her fiercely. "So just shut up, okay? If you rat us out, I'll tell Mom about yesterday."

"But you don't know anything about yester—" she began before she realized he was talking about her absence from school and gulped back her words. "You just surprised me. Wow. You look so old, like real soldiers—"

Ray saluted. "One hundred and sixth New York, at your service!"

Molly took a breath. "You look great," she said hesitantly. "But—what're you doing? I mean, I thought Dad and Mom said you, um—couldn't go."

"Yeah, but they can just—"

"Chill, Robbie," said Ray soothingly. He turned to his sisters. "Look, it's totally not fair, because he *did* it, the paper, I mean. Just 'cause Dad doesn't think it's, like, *worthy*, it's totally not fair to say he didn't do it. And they *said* he could go if he finished, which he did at, like, two a.m. So we're going," he concluded.

Miri was watching Robbie. "I didn't think you liked reenacting *that* much. I mean, enough to get in trouble for."

"You don't know," he said, lifting his chin defiantly. "First, Mom's all like, you gotta do this reenactment, and then they're all, you can't do it. I don't care. They're total a—" Even in his fury, he couldn't bring himself to say it. "Jerks."

"How're you going to get there?" Molly asked.

"Mr. Emory," said Ray promptly. "He says he'll give us a ride from Boyce, and that's only two miles. I looked on the map."

"We can walk two miles," said Robbie.

"I meant, how are you going to get out of here?" Molly said.

"Dad's out back, right?" said Ray, with the air of someone who had done research.

"And Mom's shopping," said Robbie. "So, easy—"
He opened the front door with a flourish. And then shut it quickly. "Fritz."

"Are the kids out there, too?" asked Ray, exasperated.

"Yup," said Miri. "And you know how much they like to tell on people."

Ray and Robbie looked at each other bitterly. "And Dad's in the back," muttered Ray. "We're prisoners in our own house."

"This is totally not fair!" said Robbie. "This is nuts!" He paced the hallway like a tiger in a cage.

Miri and Molly looked at each other and edged toward the kitchen. They didn't want to be around when he blew his top. He usually threw things.

But as they settled back to work, they heard, not an explosion, but a laugh. "Sweet!" exclaimed Ray.

There was a pause, and then they heard Robbie say, very softly, "Bye."

What? Molly and Miri turned to look at each other. Bye? "Guys?" called Miri. From the front hall came silence.

Suddenly, Molly shoved back her chair. "Guys!" she yelled, running, "Guys! Ray! Robbie! Oh nonono! *Miri!*"

But Miri was already at her side. Together, their hearts like lead, they stared at the gaping hole in the side of the living room. Where the plastic tarp had been shoved aside, they could see out into the bright golden trees and the wheeling blackberry bushes. They could hear the buzz of their father's drill and the efficient snap of Fritz's clippers. For a moment, the two girls looked at their simple, normal, beautiful world.

And then they climbed up on the jagged edge of the wall and jumped out of it.

⌁ CHAPTER ⌁

11

"THEY MUST HAVE NOTICED *some*thing," said Molly, crunching over fallen leaves.

Miri nodded. It seemed impossible that her brothers could have traveled so far into the woods without noticing the complete lack of neighbors and cars and houses. Or the number of trees that would have had to spring up overnight to account for the thick forest they were moving through. Or the eerie silence that hung over everything. But what she said was, "They don't pay attention to how things look."

"They're morons," muttered Molly.

Miri nodded again. They were morons. They paid no attention. They goofed around, they didn't do their homework, they galloped around battlefields thinking it was a video game. They lied, they teased, they yelled, they tiptoed into the kitchen on their gigantic feet, sprigs of hair bursting from under their caps, their eyes shining. "We got you guys something," whispered Robbie, his hands cupped carefully around the dirtiest T-shirt in the world. "A present. Because of yesterday." Miri's heart tightened. And Robbie again, his blue eyes huge in the dim light. "I don't see how they could do it," he was saying. "Fight like that, I mean. I couldn't." He couldn't. She had to save him. Both of them.

But how? Where could they be? At the bottom of the long, sloping field in front of the 1860s version of their house, the two girls had paused and, in order to choose their direction, tried to think like Ray and Robbie. After a few moments, they'd concluded that choosing randomly would be the same as thinking like their brothers, and they'd turned left. Since then, they'd trudged through a long, monotonous series of fields and woods, all of them the same brownish-green color in the smoke-smelling afternoon. Miri shivered, only partly from the chilly breeze. Where *were* they? What could have happened to them?

Molly stopped. "We should have found them by now."

Miri hadn't wanted to say it. She surveyed the trees, bushes, and weeds around her. They looked like all the other trees, bushes, and weeds she'd seen in the past two hours. "You don't think—I mean, they couldn't have, but—you don't think they could've run into an actual *battle*, do you?"

"If there were a battle close enough for them to have run into, I think we would have heard it," Molly said at once, and Miri could tell that she had been worrying about the same thing. "Remember how loud it was?"

Miri nodded, listening to the silence. "Yeah. I guess we just keep going."

They hiked on, more anxious than ever. Trees, a creek, a rolling field. More trees. A fence. Trees, trees, trees, a rolling field. Trees. A fence with a rolling field on the other side—

Suddenly, Molly's hand gripped Miri's arm. Beyond the fence, at end of the field, was a man on horseback. He hadn't seen them. His back was toward them, and he made no movement. He was simply sitting in the saddle, looking into the woods.

"Should we ask if he's seen them?" murmured Miri.

"Wait a sec," Molly breathed.

Miri craned her neck, straining to get a better glimpse through her glasses. There was a slight creak as the man shifted a little in the saddle, and as he did, Miri saw the long shape of a gun lying across his lap. "Let's get out of here," she whispered.

"Listen," whispered Molly at the same moment.

Miri listened. The light breeze, which had brought the creak of the man's saddle to her ears, carried the rattle of leaves and the patient wuffle of the horse's breath. Then she heard a faint "Shut up!"

The man had heard it, too. He straightened and raised his rifle in one smooth movement.

"*I wanna eat eat eat—*" bellowed Ray, backing out of the trees at a run.

"*Monkey fooood!*" chorused Robbie, loping after him. "*I wanna eat—*" He stopped, his face brightening at the sight of the man on horseback. "Hi! Hey! Good! Are we there? We're so dang lost, man!"

Ray turned, tripping over his own legs as he did so. "Cool dude! You got a gun! Whoa!" The horse whinnied in alarm as the boys gangled toward her. "Where'd you get the horse? They didn't give *us* a horse. Where's Mr. Emory?"

"We're with him. Mr. Emory," said Robbie, gazing up at the man in the saddle.

The man laughed, high and excited, and Miri's mouth went dry. She'd know that laugh anywhere.

"No," she moaned under her breath. "Not Carter."

Run away, her mind pleaded. *Run, run, run, NOW.* But her brothers stood trustingly beside Carter's horse.

Molly gripped Miri's arm with white knuckles. "We could charge him," she whispered. "We'll run right at him and scream, and maybe the horse will shy—" She started forward.

"No!" Miri yanked her back. "He's got a gun! He'll shoot us for sure—you know he will!"

Carter was still laughing. "Union's pretty hard up, I guess, drafting nits like you. We'll win this war yet."

"What?" said Robbie. As usual, he didn't wait for an answer. "You seen Mr. Emory?"

"You're with General Emory?" Carter's voice rose. "Why, that's the best news I've heard all day. And would you look at that!" He craned his head forward. "A matched set! I'll be damned! Congratulations, boys. You are the answer to my prayers—or you would be, if I prayed. Two prisoners of war, matched and made to order, to replace the ones I mislaid yesterday! Ha!" He cackled gleefully, and Miri and Molly looked at each other, shaken. Replacement prisoners? Their own brothers were replacements for Jamie and his uncle? "Now," Carter was saying, "are you two going to come along easy or are you going to put up a fight?"

"Where are we going?" demanded Ray. "We're supposed to get a ride with Mr. Emory."

"Shut up, boy," said Carter irritably. "You talk too much. Move. Ahead of me."

Miri tensed. She knew what was coming. Dozens—possibly hundreds—of safety lectures had pounded in one simple message: Never, ever go anywhere with a stranger. Her brothers were about to put their training into action. *Don't*, she begged them silently.

But they did. Ray straightened and took a step backward. "No, thanks," he said, as recommended. "We'll stick to our own plan."

"What?" Carter said in disbelief.

Robbie moved to stand alongside his brother. "We'll be going now," he said in the deepest voice he could manage.

Carter leaned down from his saddle and cracked Robbie across the face with the butt of his rifle, sending him sprawling in the grass.

"*Hey!*" yelled Ray, backing away. "What the heck are you doing, man? Oh! Whoa! You're not supposed to do that!" He knelt beside his brother and then looked up at Carter in horror. "That's blood!"

"My *God*!" roared Carter. "Why is it my fate to encounter *imbeciles*? What have I done to you, Lord, that you should serve me this way? Get up, you wretched clot, and get the other on his feet, and *march*. You are a prisoner of war! Get up, or I'll whip you down the road before me like a mule. Get *up*!"

Ray's eyes were wide as he helped Robbie to his feet. Dazed, Robbie took a wheeling step and fell again. Once more, Ray heaved him up until they both stood, unsteadily, before Carter.

Miri's hand went to her mouth and Molly's did the same. Robbie's face was streaming blood.

"Through the gate," ordered Carter.

"But he can't," stammered Ray. "Walk, I mean. Not yet, anyway. Look at—"

Carter lifted his rifle and took aim at Ray's face. Miri and Molly clutched at each other helplessly, not breathing. For a long moment, no one moved. Then Ray grabbed Robbie by the arm, turned him around, and propelled him into a staggering step toward the gate. "It's another miracle cure," Carter said sourly and nudged his horse forward.

. . .

The two girls followed. At first, they attempted to move without making a sound, but that proved both impossible and time-consuming, and they nearly lost sight of the threesome ahead of them. Pretty soon, they decided to give up on silence and concentrate on speed. No one gave any sign of noticing. Carter, on horseback, demanded that the boys keep up with his pace, and they struggled to obey. Trailing fifty feet behind, Miri saw Ray wrap his arm around Robbie to hold him upright, a gesture so unthinkably unlike him that it scared her more than anything that had happened yet.

Stay alive, stay alive, she ordered them. She had used the same words the day before, commanding Jamie to live. And see, she encouraged herself, that had worked out. Yeah, right. It hadn't worked out very well for Ray and Robbie. Ugh. Don't think about that. Think about getting Robbie and Ray away from Carter. She reviewed the possibilities. They could attack. Surely, the four of them—but no, that was ridiculous. Carter had a gun and a horse. Plus, she thought, remembering his steel-trap fingers, he was probably stronger than the four of them put together. And if he caught sight of Miri or Molly, he'd be more than happy to shoot them as payback for the day before.

"We could throw a rock at him," Molly said under her breath.

"We'd have to bean him," Miri muttered, "and if we missed, he'd know we were here." No, attack was out. They'd have to outwit him. When they got wherever it was they were going, Miri and Molly would—what? Do something. Miri tried to think of a plan and came up blank. Maybe Molly would think of something. Maybe some big Yankee with a gun would rescue them. In the meantime, there was nothing to do but follow and hope that they wouldn't be discovered. And hope that Robbie was okay. And hope that they'd be able to get back to the house and the twenty-first century again. And hope that they wouldn't run into some battle on the way. *Hope's cheap*, commented her brain. *And guess why? Because it's not worth anything.* Who asked you? she retorted.

∻ CHAPTER ∻

12

SOME HOURS LATER, the girls were crouched in the shadow of a small wooden structure—an outhouse, from the smell of it—taking turns peering at a patch of lumpy grass in the distance.

Robbie was lying on it. They knew this because they could see one of his shoulders and the top of his head. The rest of him, all of Ray, and most important, the whereabouts of Carter, were blocked by the corner of a big white house jutting into their view.

Robbie was lying very still.

"Probably he's just resting," Miri whispered for the sixth time.

"But where's Ray?" hissed Molly. Miri stretched

her head as far forward as she dared and got a glimpse of Robbie's other shoulder. "You think they took him someplace?"

Miri could only shake her head. There was no way to know. After the torturous walk, they'd been relieved to see the fields give way to a wide road and then a house or two. A short time later, Carter directed his prisoners toward something that looked almost like a village—a few buildings clumped together—and then turned them down a dirt lane leading to the big white house. Miri and Molly had ducked from tree to tree to outhouse, keeping their brothers in sight until they saw Carter pull his horse to a halt and dismount. At that, they, too, came to halt, stuck at the back of the outhouse as first Carter and then Ray disappeared from view around the white corner. After a moment, Robbie lay down on the ground. That was all, for a long time. So Miri and Molly waited, twitching at every sound, peering at Robbie's head, telling each other he was okay, and trying to make a plan.

"I'm pretty sure he's just resting," said Miri worriedly.

"This is crazy," muttered Molly. "We should just

go get him. I'm going to go get him." She started forward—and jumped back again as Carter's enormous figure appeared beside Robbie, prodding him with his boot.

Robbie didn't move.

Carter frowned, considered, and then kicked him in the ribs. Robbie groaned and curled into a ball. Carter looked up, toward the house. "He's alive!" he called. "So that's two!" He walked jauntily away.

Two prisoners. Two replacements for Jamie and his uncle. Miri felt slightly sick. She and Molly had made this happen or, at least, allowed it to happen. To think that she had been so proud the night before that she had saved Jamie. She hadn't given a moment's thought to what the older man had said— "You can get yourself some other boys, easy." That was what Carter had done: He'd gotten her brothers. Easy. And if it hadn't been them, she reminded herself, it would have been someone else's brothers.

"We did this," she muttered to Molly.

"I know we did," Molly said. "And now we have to undo it."

We have to undo it. But how? Okay, Miri told

herself, the good news is that we know Robbie's alive. But what about Ray? And where are they going to be taken? We should just go for it, she decided. We should stop waffling and go for it. And then Carter will kill us. Okay, we'll wait, she decided. We'll wait and see what happens. But they might take the guys somewhere we can't get them. We should go for it, she decided. But Carter. But—

"Mir?" Molly interrupted her thoughts.

"What?"

"Look at the house."

"The *house*?" Who cared about the house?

"Yeah, the house," whispered Molly. "And look up the road that way." She pointed. "Does it look familiar?"

Impatiently, Miri turned to glance at the house. White, columns, long windows, big. So what? The road. Church, some kind of barn, store, house, big deal.

Wait. Miri squinted at the church. White. A bowl-shaped dome thing on top. A cemetery in the back. She swung quickly back to the house. Long windows with fans of glass at the top. Lots of low buildings behind. A wide front yard.

"Oh my gosh," she breathed. "It's Paxton."

In their own time, Paxton was a small, tired town featuring the usual assortment of fast-food restaurants, church thrift shops, insurance offices, grocery stores, and an out-of-place organic herbalist. But on a sign at the edge of town, it called itself PAXTON, DREAM OF THE OLD DOMINION, which meant it had been around for a long time. Every fifth grader within forty miles had to go on a field trip to view the historic sights of Paxton, consisting of a well, a piece of a jail, a church, and the Buckley House. At the Buckley House, nice ladies in hoopskirts showed them shiny old furniture, so it was generally considered to be the winner of the Field Trip Boredom Sweepstakes. In Miri and Molly's year, a kid on his second round of fifth grade and therefore his second round of the historic sights of Paxton, had tried to set the house afire. While this had added some temporary zest to the field trip, the ensuing teacher/policeman/firefighter frenzy had lasted all afternoon, giving Miri and Molly's class what their teacher later called a priceless opportunity to become experts in the architecture of the Buckley House.

And here it was, right in front of them. Dingier and dirtier than it was in the twenty-first century, but definitely the Buckley House.

"It's Paxton. We're in Paxton," whispered Molly jubilantly. "We know where we are."

Miri nodded, speechless with gratitude. *Thank you*, she said to the heavens. *Thank you*. It was their first piece of good luck. They knew Paxton. Paxton was three miles from their house. Three straight miles with landmarks that included a creek to keep them on the right path. She let out a long breath. It's going to be okay, she told herself. It's going to be fine. All they had to do was get the boys and run like crazy for the woods. If they moved fast, they'd have a decent head start. They'd dive into the woods, follow the creek, and get back to the house and the precious front door that would lead them home.

Her eyes fell on Robbie, motionless on the grass. She wondered if he could run at all, much less like crazy.

Molly followed her gaze. "Look," she said, "Let's just *try* it. We're never going to get anywhere standing here staring at Robbie's head."

Miri nodded. "You're right." That was Molly—always ready to take action, to move forward. I should be braver, Miri thought. Bolder. *Oh yeah?* inquired her enemy brain. *Like yesterday? When you attacked Carter and started this whole mess?* Her brain was right, she decided. She should be more careful. "What about Carter?"

Molly considered Robbie, still lying S-shaped on the grass where Carter had left him. "Look," she said, turning back to Miri. "He was talking to someone, right?" Miri nodded. "So there's someone else around. Someone watching! And Carter can't do anything to us if someone else is watching. Remember Hern? Hern said he couldn't hurt two little girls! That's us," she added. "Two little girls."

"You're right!" agreed Miri, and, re-emboldened, she stepped out from behind the outhouse.

"Hey!" Molly said in an agonized whisper. "Get back here! Roll up your pants! You've got to look like a girl!"

Whoops! Miri ducked quickly back into the outhouse shadow. "We should take our glasses off, too, I think," she said as she yanked on her jeans and smoothed down her T-shirt into a more ladylike shape. "I've never seen an olden-days girl with glasses." Molly nodded and dropped her glasses into her pocket. Miri, doing the same, sighed as she entered the world of smear.

Now they were ready. Cautiously this time, they stepped into open territory—and paused, waiting to be caught. Nothing. Dead quiet. Carefully, slowly, their footsteps soft in the dirt, they crept toward the house. Nobody appeared. Nobody cried out, "Who are you? Stop!" The house stood still and silent in the pale afternoon light. They sidled along the wall—Miri noted that an awful lot of magic consisted of sidling along walls—until they reached the white brick corner that had been blocking their view for the last hour, and finally saw what lay beyond.

On a wide, weedy circle of grass, Ray was sitting beside Robbie's curled back. As they watched, he leaned over his brother, eyed his head worriedly, and then slumped back into his original position.

Carter was nowhere to be seen.

Miri and Molly looked at each other, nodded, and moved in unison out onto the lawn. "Ray!" called Miri, low.

He whirled around, and even without glasses, she could see the relief flooding over his face. "Miri! Robbie's—" he began.

"What in *tarnation* you think yer doing?" squawked a voice.

All three of them froze. Slowly, the two girls turned to face the Buckley House. There, on the porch, a man in uniform sat beside a white column, an unmistakable long pistol clutched in his hand. "*You* gals, you just get yourselves right-a-here this minute!" he bellowed indignantly.

Miri's eyes locked on Ray's. Don't say anything, she mouthed. He gave a tiny nod.

The guard, red-faced and scowling, watched them approach. "You coulda got shot, running out there like that, and you wouldn't have a soul to blame but yer own selves. What you got in your heads? Stuffing?"

"Eggs!" cried Molly merrily. Miri goggled at her. Eggs? Molly babbled on, "My mama's old hen laid sixteen eggs in the last four days, and Mama says it's a testament to the miraculous ways of Providence they didn't get eaten by a fox 'cause she hid one—that's the hen, not Mama—all the way under the porch, and Mama says we got to offer the Lord's bounty to our fighting boys before the Yankees get 'em—that's the eggs, not the boys—so she sent us on over here to ask if y'all want to buy 'em—some eggs, that is—for a nickel. Apiece." She ran out of breath.

Miri almost burst into applause. Eggs! How did Molly think of things like that? And how did she manage to act so real? She didn't stutter or hesitate. She sounded like a 100 percent genuine 1860s girl. And it worked! The scowling guard was smiling.

"You are right talkative, child," he said. "Yer tongue gonna fall plumb outta yer head if you go on like that."

Molly giggled. "That's just exactly what Mama says. Mama says a lady's voice is ever gentle and low, an excellent thing in a woman, but no one can hear you if your voice is ever gentle and—"

The soldier interrupted, "You said you got eggs?"

Molly nodded. "We got sixteen, but Mama ate two and put by two for me'n'her"—she poked her chin in Miri's direction—"and then she gave two to Dr. Purdy 'cause he came when Mama thought I had the scarlet fever—which I didn't—and she didn't have a cent at the time, and all that leaves ten and that's what we want to know if you want. For only five cents apiece, which is real good, because we heard they sold 'em for twenty-five cents up in Boyce last week."

The man was laughing now. "I don't see how you ever had time to swallow an egg, all the jabbering you do. I tell you what, girl, Mrs. Hibbs—" Suddenly, he stopped and glared over Molly's shoulder. "You just set yourself right back down, soldier, or I'll make you sorry you didn't."

Miri turned to see Ray standing uncertainly in the grass. Though his face was a blur, Miri knew he was looking to her and Miri, hoping for direction. Behind her back, Miri spread her fingers and gestured toward the ground: Sit down. He sat down.

"You don't need no eggs nohow!" the guard called. "You'll be dead by morning!"

Miri felt the blood drain from her face.

"Well, looka you!" he said with concern. "You gone white as a sheet. You tenderhearted?"

Speechless, Miri nodded. Dead by morning?

"Aw, don't fret," the soldier comforted her.

"They're Yankees. Same regiment as killed our boys over in Front Royal. Killed 'em in cold blood and now the Colonel aims to pay 'em back." He nodded at her encouragingly, certain she would be cheered by this news.

"The Colonel's going to—he's going to—" Miri's mouth couldn't quite form the words.

"Hang 'em, I think." The guard scratched his chin with the butt of his gun. "Maybe shoot 'em."

"They look awful young," Molly croaked.

The guard squinted at the two figures on the lawn, and Miri realized glumly that compared with most of the Civil War soldiers she'd seen, her brothers were tall and healthy-looking. "Nah," he said. "Look at 'em. They're in the ranks, ain't they? They're old enough. One of those boys they killed over at Front Royal wasn't hardly seventeen. He wasn't even *in* the dang army, and they killed him just the same." He glanced at Ray and Robbie once more, shrugged, and returned to the important subject. "Now, I would partake of an egg with a glad heart, 'cause I ain't had enough to eat today—nor yesterday, now that I think of it—but Mrs. Hibbs, she'd run me through with a red-hot poker if I ate up the Colonel's breakfast." He sighed. "She's right inside there." He nodded to the front door. "Y'all can go in."

"Mrs. Hibbs," repeated Molly, somewhat numbly. "Yes, sir." She cleared her throat. "We'll go on in."

Miri cast an agonized look over her shoulder. Turning her back seemed like a betrayal. Was she seeing her brothers for the last time?

"Go on!" urged the guard. There was nothing else to do. Like robots, the two girls climbed the stairs. Behind them, the guard settled back against the column. "Say, boys, you hungry?" he yelled toward Ray and Robbie.

Silence.

"I say are you boys hungry?"

"Yeah," Ray said.

"Well, don't you fret!" chortled the guard. "After tomorrow, you won't be hungry no more!"

The two girls entered the hallway, and Molly stopped, breathing hoarsely. "What're we going to do?" she whispered. She gripped Miri's shoulder. "What're we going to *do*?"

"Something," Miri said. "I don't know what, but something."

Molly lifted her head, and Miri saw panic in her eyes. "Tomorrow. They're going to hang them *tomorrow*." Her fingers tightened. "If it were me instead of them, it'd be easy. I wouldn't care, but it's them, and it's our fault and I don't know what to do!"

She's scared, Miri realized with surprise. Molly's scared. She wants to make a decision, to take action, to fix the problem, but she's scared she's going to do the wrong thing. Most of the time, discovering Molly's fear would have doubled Miri's own. But now it made her feel protective. She found Molly's hand and squeezed it. "Listen," she said. "I'll think of a way. You talk to Mrs. Hibbs about eggs and let me think. I'll find us a way out of this. I promise."

Molly's hunched shoulders relaxed a tiny bit. She nodded and took a quaking breath. "Mrs. Hibbs?" she called into the gloom of the hallway. "Mrs. Hibbs?"

Meanwhile, Miri brought her knuckle to her mouth and began to chew, her standard problem-solving procedure. Munching, she encouraged herself. Haven't we always found a way before? Haven't we always been able to figure out how to make the magic work the way we needed it to?

"What are you two ragamuffins doing in my house?" exclaimed a harsh voice. "You can just go on your way, you hear? You're tracking up my carpet, lookit that!" A tiny woman who looked as though she'd been carved from wood hurried into the hall, her beady eyes glaring.

"Uh, Mrs. Hibbs?" stammered Molly. "I got some—"

"Out!" The woman whisked them away with tiny, sticklike fingers. "Shoo!"

Miri ignored her and continued thinking. What do I already know about magic? I know that it wants to set things right. So it doesn't want Ray and Robbie to die. Magic is on our side, she reminded herself. It's always given us the pieces and we've always figured out what to do with them. Okay, so what are the pieces?

"Mama said to tell you that they are some mighty fresh eggs," Molly was saying breathlessly, "and a nickel apiece ain't so very much, considering as how they were asking twenty-five cents up at Boyce last week. And Mama said seeing as how you got company, you might—"

"Hush! You just hush up about my company,"

hissed Mrs. Hibbs, whisking her stick-finger again.

Bossy old cow, isn't she? thought Miri inconsequentially. Then: Stop that! Think about magic!

"How many?" snapped Mrs. Hibbs.

"How many what?" asked Molly, confused.

"How many eggs, you blockhead!" snapped Mrs. Hibbs.

Who does she remind me of? Miri thought, distracted again. Someone I saw recently. Just a few days ago. Someone rude. Who was it?

Her wayward train of thought came to another stop as a door opened at the far end of the hall, and a small, thin man in a gray uniform poked his head out. With a jolt, Miri recognized the Colonel, much shorter and less impressive off a horse than on. "Betsy? What's the fuss?" he asked, looking worried.

Mrs. Hibbs's face grew pink, and her long chin cracked into a smile. "Why, Colonel!" she cried. "Don't disturb yourself! I'm just getting you some eggs for your breakfast! These children are just as filthy as Gypsies, but they say they have eggs!"

Boy, the Gypsies sure get a rotten deal, Miri

mused. Everyone blames them for everything. Just the other day, someone was yapping about Gypsies. Who? Now stop that! she scolded herself again. You're supposed to be thinking; you're supposed to be finding a way out. Magic gives us the pieces, and we have to figure out how to use them. So the pieces are—

"But I'd trade with the devil himself for you, Colonel," said Mrs. Hibbs coyly. Toothpick eyelashes fluttered.

Flutter, flutter, snickered Miri internally. Flutter, flutter, aren't you a card?

What?

Who said that?

Stop it! Find a solution! *Concentrate.*

Flutter, flutter, aren't you a card?

Flo. That's who it was. Mrs. Hibbs reminds me of Flo, fluttering at Pat Gardner.

Stop dithering! Concentrate. Magic gives us the pieces, and we have to figure out how to use them. The pieces are Carter. Ugh. The pieces are Carter, the Colonel, Jamie and his uncle, Hern, I guess, and, well, 1918. . . .

Flo's voice, sugary sweet: now, I want to show

you something I just know you'll be interested in, a military man like you.

Miri's brow wrinkled. What was it she showed him? Some kind of letter?

She gave her knuckle a particularly hard bite. Stop thinking about Flo! Think about now!

But Flo's sticky sweet voice kept coming: See? It's a safe-conduct. See? Bearer must in no way and for no purpose be detained from the pursuit of his duties. Let neither his costume nor his demeanor cause his arrest. He is in my service. General R. E. Lee.

Wait.

What was that?

Bearer must in no way and for no purpose be detained from the pursuit of his duties. Let neither his costume nor his demeanor cause his arrest. He is in my service. General R. E. Lee.

And inside Miri, there was a great silent burst of light.

It was a safe-conduct. A free pass. An escape hatch.

If they could get it, it would save Ray and Robbie.

"Flo," she gasped. "It's Flo!" All eyes, including

the Colonel's, turned to her, but Miri didn't notice. Grabbing Molly's hand, she said again, urgently, "Flo!"

"Flo?" repeated the Colonel, baffled.

"Why, yes! Flo, that's what we call her, our hen, I mean," Molly exclaimed, giving Miri a look that said What's wrong with you? "My sister just loves that chicken to distraction—"

"Ha!" yelped Miri wildly, relief of a thousand different kinds surging through her. Ray and Robbie would be saved! The pass was an order from the commander of the army. The Colonel would have to obey. And Molly! She was saved as well! They had been sent to 1918 to hear Flo flutter at Pat Gardner, not to lose Molly! Now it was clear. Now it was certain! Molly was meant to be her twin forever! "We did it!" she crowed. But wait! They hadn't done it yet. They hadn't done anything yet! To get the pass, they had to go to 1918. And to get to 1918, they had to go home. And to get home, they had to—"We have to go!" she yelled.

"Is that child having a fit?" demanded Mrs. Hibbs.

"Well," said Molly cautiously, "she might be."

Miri tried to pull herself together. She offered what she hoped was a charming, girlish smile. "Oh, no! Nonono! No fits here!" Mrs. Hibbs drew back as though she'd seen a snake, obviously not charmed, so Miri whirled around to the Colonel. "Sir! We're going to run and get you some nice eggs. Nice, nice eggs! You'll love them! Yum! So! We have to go!" Improvising, she saluted. And then again, for good measure. "See you later!" She smiled as hard as she could.

The Colonel almost—but not quite—smiled back. "Permission to retreat granted."

· · ·

She almost fell over the soldier on the front porch.

"Watch where yer going, you loony-tic!" he sputtered.

"Just running to get those eggs!" stammered Molly, throwing Miri a look that said *Chill!* "For the Colonel."

"Gonna break 'em, galloping around like that," he grumbled.

But Miri, charging toward the lawn, paid him no mind. Her eyes were on her brothers, and before the guard could stop her or order her away, she flung herself down on her knees beside them, clasping her hands together as though she were praying. "Shut up, don't say anything," she hissed. "Pretend you're praying, and we might get away with it."

Robbie opened his eyes. "Is that Miri?"

"What the *heck* is going on—" Ray burst out in a whisper.

"Shh. Pray! Look like you're praying! We have to go away but only for a while. We're going to try—there's a way to get you out, but we have to go home and get it first—"

"Get away from them Yankees, girl! How many times do I have to tell you?" The soldier was rising to his feet.

"I'm praying for their souls!" Miri yelled over her shoulder. Then, as fast as she could, "Listen, guys, just do whatever they tell you. Don't argue with them, especially not Carter—he's the big, mean one—just do what he says, and we'll find you. But if they take you somewhere, try to leave a message, drop something, a trail or something, so we know where you—"

"Tarnation child, get up!"

He was coming closer, Molly's voice alongside rising, "—she's real religious, always praying, she don't mean anything by it, really!"

Robbie gazed at her sleepily. "My head hurts."

Miri's eyes met Ray's. "We'll be back. I promise."

"Is this real?" he asked under his breath.

She nodded and rose to her feet, turning to face the soldier bearing down on her with Molly at his side, babbling anxiously, "Pray, pray, pray, all day, all night. She's just like that!"

Miri arranged her face into the most spiritual expression she could manage and said solemnly, "Amen."

"Amen," echoed Molly.

"*Humph!*" sniffed the guard. "Git!"

With one last look at Ray and Robbie, they got.

MIRI EXPLAINED IT TO MOLLY in gasps as they ran. Flo, Pat Gardner, the safe-conduct signed by R. E. Lee.

Molly stopped. "But we can't get ahold of it. We can't get to 1918, remember?"

Miri bent double, her hands on her knees. "There's got to be a way," she panted. "I'll do anything. If we knock over one of Ollie's posts, maybe the old porch will come back. There's got to be a way. That's why we were sent to 1918. I know it."

Molly straightened. For a moment she looked away, into the woods. When she turned back to Miri, her face was pale. She looked intently at Miri. "We were sent there to hear about the safe-conduct?"

Miri nodded.

"So we could save Ray and Robbie?"

Miri nodded.

"Not so I could keep Maudie and Pat from meeting?"

Miri nodded.

Another pause. "So I don't have to—" Molly was talking softly, almost to herself. "I don't have to give you up?" She lifted her eyes to Miri's. "Really?"

"Really. You're supposed to be my sister; you're supposed to be one of us," Miri said.

She watched as a secret fear, cold and tight as an ice cube, melted away from her sister's face. Then Molly gave a short, firm nod. "Okay," she said, her voice clear and strong. "Okay, then. We'll get that pass. No matter what it takes."

Miri couldn't help grinning at the unstoppable determination in her voice. "Hi again," she said. "It's nice to have you back."

But after that, they just ran. They ran and ran and ran. Miri hadn't known she could run for that long. A personal record, she thought, ducking under a stringy branch. Coach Vargas would be proud. Too bad I can't tell him.

When they finally emerged from the cover of trees, the half-size, Civil War version of the house was in sight, with its crushed and dangling porch. They pounded toward it. All they had to do was go through the door and they'd be home. They flew up the stairs.

"Wait." On the porch, Miri bent double again, panting.

Molly, gasping herself, gave a questioning look.

"Want to test it," Miri panted, not very informatively. "That." She pointed to the hole in the porch floor, where the mangled wood ended in a cliff hanging over empty air. "Looks like it got bombed."

"Shelled," said Molly. "That's what they called it."

"Whatever. It's a hole in the house, isn't it? Which means it's a hole in time. It'll take us somewhere, maybe to 1918," Miri said.

Molly shook her head. "Can't. 1918 is forward."

"It could go in both directions," said Miri.

Molly looked at the broken-off edge suspiciously. "I don't think so," she said. "Don't jump into it, okay?"

"Why not? I can just come in the door again," said Miri. She sidled around the precarious floorboards that curved, in a sort of half-circle rim, around the hole. "We've got to try everything, don't we?" She leaned over. She could see the stubbly ground below. "There's just grass down there—"

And then she was pulled to her knees by a force

stronger than gravity. She cried out, madly teetering on the wooden precipice, her hands scrabbling at empty air. She was falling, the earth below rushing toward her. Down she went, catching a flashing glimpse of the view beneath floor-level—trees pressed close to the house, very close, very dark, swaying angrily in the wind—and then two arms circled her middle, and she found herself slammed backward, hard.

She lay there, gasping and shaking. "Wow," she said when she could speak. "I almost—almost—" Her voice cracked. "That was scary."

"What was it?" Molly asked.

Miri shivered. "Trees. Lots of them, really close. Like a forest. But—but—that wasn't the scary part."

Molly waited.

Miri looked fearfully toward the abrupt edge of wood. "The scary part was how much it wanted me to fall in." She shivered. "Why? Why would it want that?"

Molly thought for a moment. "I don't think the magic started with the house." Her eyes met Miri's. "I think the magic started with the place. The house just happened to be built on top of it." She glanced almost fearfully at the dangling floorboards. "I think there's something really old down there. Old magic is the purest. The most undiluted. We don't know what it wants."

Miri nodded, still staring at the hole. It showed no sign of what was inside. It looked completely innocent. Well, maybe not innocent, since it was made by a war, but explainable. Within the circle of history. Not like what she had just seen. The circle of history was tiny compared to the circle of time.

"There's going to be a point when we won't be able to get home," said Molly quietly. "There's a time before the house. If we go there, there's no way back."

Miri shivered again. "I think," she said, trying to steady herself, "that we should find another way to get to 1918."

Molly nodded. "On to Plan B."

• • •

Plan B was simple. If Ollie's perimeter of posts had blocked the time-tunnel to 1918, then destroying the perimeter would open it again. To punch a hole in time, all they had to do was knock down a single post. But knocking down Ollie's posts proved to be more difficult than they had thought. Scrambling through the woods, Miri had imagined that a good, strong slam would dislodge a post from its hole. Wrong. A good, strong slam practically broke her arm. Ollie was sort of weird, but he built his porches to last. He didn't just jam a post in the ground and build a porch on top of it. Nope. He stuck his posts into the ground with concrete. After Miri had finished hissing hurt-arm bad words, the girls decided to try breaking up the concrete with their father's pickaxe. If they smashed the concrete to powder and *then* slammed, the post would surely fall.

Miri glanced up, toward the kitchen above her head. She couldn't believe that her parents hadn't heard her bad words. Or Molly dropping the pickaxe. But apparently they hadn't. No one was looking out the window, anyway. What if I were a burglar? she thought. "Go," she said.

With a grunt, Molly heaved the pickaxe up and over. It bounced off the concrete.

Miri inspected it hopefully. Not even a crack. "Try again."

"Yow! That hurts," Molly winced as the pickaxe boinged up again.

"That darn Ollie," said Miri. "You didn't even make a dent. Try the crowbar."

"You."

"Okay. Keep an eye on the window."

They traded places. Miri jammed the crowbar into the shallow trench they had dug next to the hunk of concrete. She managed to get the iron bar about two inches below the surface of the earth. Then she pressed it into the side of the concrete block and stomped on the other end.

It didn't budge. Miri tried again. Nothing. It didn't feel like magic. It felt like construction work.

"What time do you think it is?" Molly muttered, looking at the sun.

"Three, three thirty. Don't look at the sky, look at the window," Miri said crabbily. She whacked the concrete with the crowbar.

"This isn't working," said Molly. "Got any other ideas?"

Miri flung the crowbar to the ground. "No."

Molly rubbed her head. "I always think you're going to come up with some brilliant idea."

"I always think you're going to make some brilliant move," Miri sighed. "I don't have any ideas."

"I don't have any moves," said Molly.

Forlornly, they listened to the passing of the afternoon.

Then Molly began to turn in a slow circle. "Will you help us?" she asked softly of the house, the grass, the trees. "We need you to show us what to do."

"Please," Miri said, holding out her arms. "Just give us a hint, and we'll take it from there. Give us one tiny piece."

They paused, but there was no answer, just a little breeze that curled through the trees, rustling the golden-green leaves.

"You can't want Ray and Robbie to die," Molly begged. "That can't be what you think is right."

A waft of air lifted her hair.

"Thanks. A breeze. That's helpful," Miri said bitterly. "Stupid wind." She pulled a wayward elm leaf out of her hair. "Stupid trees, stupid leaves."

"Wait," said Molly. She snatched the leaf as it spiraled to the ground. "Maybe—that *is* the hint." She gazed at the bit of green. "It's from the elm."

Miri looked at it. It was an elm leaf. "So?"

There was a pause. Then Molly looked up, her smile radiant. "In 1918, there was a tree house in the elm. Now it's gone. There's a hole in time, and it's up in the elm tree. Bet you anything."

Miri looked at the little leaf. "Thank you," she called to the world. And then, just in case the magic was touchy, "Sorry I said you were stupid."

. . .

Plan B, Part Two, was getting rid of Mom and Dad. Whacking pickaxes on concrete in the backyard without anyone noticing required luck, but dragging a ladder to the middle of the front yard, climbing into the elm tree, and then disappearing without anyone noticing required a lie.

". . . Plus, it'll explain why Ray and Robbie are missing," Molly was saying.

"Right." Miri nodded. "I know. But still."

"We have to," said Molly.

"I know. I just hate it, is all."

Molly pushed open the front door. "Hi, Mom!" she bellowed. "Hi!"

"Too loud!" whispered Miri. "Act normal!"

Mom's voice whirled out of the kitchen. "Just where have the two of you been all afternoon, might I ask?" And there she was, hands on hips, eyebrows raised. "Were you perhaps someplace where telephones have not yet been invented?" Miri choked. "Why didn't you call?"

Molly took over. "We're really sorry, Mom. We were over at Sophie's and we totally lost track of time. Gosh, we're sorry. Her mom is letting her get a tattoo."

Good one, admired Miri, as their mother was diverted into a lecture about bad decisions and future regrets. Tattoos were one of her great subjects, always ending in a description of how the butterfly of youth would look on the sagging flesh of old age. "Like fungus!" she concluded.

"You're right, Mom," said Molly. "And next time, we'll call. We're sorry." She smiled sincerely.

"Good. You'd better," said Mom. There was a pause. "Say, girls?" She was trying to sound casual, but her voice rose anxiously. "Do you know where your brothers went? No one's seen them since this morning. I knew they'd probably go off in a huff, but I thought they'd be back by now. I called that dopey Rudy they love so much, but he hadn't seen them. I even called Mr. Emory. I didn't think they'd dare disobey, but I wasn't—well, anyway, he said they'd called him for a ride, but then they didn't turn up. . . ." Her voice trailed off, and she bit her lip. "Do you have any idea where they are?"

Miri saw the worry on her mother's face and wished she didn't have to do what she was about to do. "Well," she said uncertainly. She and Molly exchanged purposely meaningful looks.

"What?" said Mom, swallowing the bait.

Molly grimaced. "Um, I think—um—well, I don't know for sure, but I *think*—maybe they went to, um, Winchester."

Miri nodded reluctantly.

"Winchester?" their mother repeated. "Why would they? *How* would they?"

"Bus," whispered Molly.

"But why? And why didn't you tell me?" demanded Mom.

"We didn't know!" Miri felt bad about protecting herself while she was throwing her brothers to the dogs, but it had to be done. "We heard about it. We heard some guy at school say that Deathbag—you know, that gross band they're into?—was playing in Winchester, and he said Ray said he and Robbie were going to take the bus, but we thought they were kidding."

"Until now," added Molly.

Their mother put her hands over her eyes. Miri

looked guiltily at Molly. "Why are they so dumb?" groaned Mom. She took her hands away from her face and asked, "Where's the band playing?"

"Well, it's Deathbag," said Miri slowly. "They only play in cemeteries." She was feeling guiltier and guiltier. Her poor parents were going to drive all the way to Winchester and go from cemetery to cemetery for nothing. They were going to be worried. They were going to be really, really worried. She felt terrible.

"Cemeteries!" wailed her mother. "How can that be legal?"

"It's not," said Molly in a small voice. "That's why they never announce it." Their parents would never check, they had decided. And Deathbag *had* played in a cemetery. Once.

"It's just a stage," their mother said. "They're thirteen years old and their judgment is impaired. It's perfectly normal." She rubbed her forehead wearily. "Probably every mom has to drive thirty miles and search through cemeteries for her sons. Right?" she asked her daughters. They nodded. "I hope so. Frank!" she called up the stairs. "Nora! Nellie! Time for a road trip!" She turned back to

Miri and Molly. "Thank you for telling me," she said and reached to pat their cheeks.

That made them feel even worse.

. . .

Ten minutes later, the van was crunching down the driveway.

"I don't think I can hold still much longer," muttered Miri. Her leg was jiggling uncontrollably—it wanted to run, to hurry, to *get*.

"Just another minute, until they get out of the driveway," said Molly through gritted teeth. Their mother turned to wave at them. They waved back.

The van pulled out into the road, and their hands dropped to their sides. "Now!"

And now for Plan B, Part Three. In no time at all, the ladder was set against the elm tree's stubbly gray trunk.

From the porch, Cookie observed their movements with concern. The humans were attempting to climb a tree. Humans didn't climb trees. Cats climbed trees. Trees were, in fact, the property of cats. No trespassers. Cookie rose to her feet and trotted out to the front yard to claim her possession.

❧ CHAPTER ❧

14

TWO-THIRDS OF THE WAY up the ladder, Miri paused and closed her eyes, trying to recollect the precise position of the tree house. The tree had been shorter then, much shorter, its branches closer to the ground. Higher than the windows on the first floor? Maybe. Lower than the windows on the second? Maybe. She climbed another rung. That high? She didn't know. There was only one way to find out.

She swung her foot out, poking the air, seeking a floor, or a wall, or even a roof—had the tree house had a roof? She couldn't remember. She had only seen it for a moment and from far away. Her foot waved uselessly through space. Miri edged to the farthest inch of the rung and poked the air again.

Nothing.

She looked down, to where Molly was waiting three rungs below. They didn't say anything. They didn't need to. Each knew what the other was thinking: What if this doesn't work? Then what?

It had to work. It *had* to. Miri climbed up to the next rung. She had only three more to go, and the top rung featured a special sign that read THIS IS NOT A STEP. Which it totally was. She would step on it anyway. Why include a rung no one can step on? she argued, as again, she swung her foot over the side of the ladder and kicked investigatively. Back and forth. This way and that. Up and—

Thonk.

She'd hit something. Something hard. Something that sounded like wood. Once again, Miri kicked. *Thonk.* She'd found it!

She leaned forward, into the void, and patted her hand cautiously—*pat, pat, pat*—there! Under her fingers, she felt a rough edge of splintering wood. It was a board. "Got it!" she said.

"Step out onto it," said Molly. "I'm right behind you."

Miri clung to the precarious ladder with one arm and stretched the other out as far as she could, seeking a surface—there! There, there, there. Now for her foot. *Pat, pat, pat*—a floor! Hmm. Hope it's wide enough, she thought. If I fall out of the tree and break my arm, which century will I fall into? What did they do with broken arms in 1918? Oh shut up, she ordered herself, and swung sideways off the ladder.

At the foot of the tree, Cookie snapped her tail back and forth to summon her energy. She began with an invigorating skitter sideways, followed by a frantic race around the tree. Then she hurled herself at the trunk, where she hung, breathing heavily, for a moment before dashing madly up the bark.

"*Cookie!*" scolded Molly. "Stop running around. You're going to—"

In a frenzy, Cookie lunged between Miri and the ladder and took a flying leap at a branch below. "Yow!" squealed both cat and girl as they fell forward into nothing and disappeared.

• • •

"Whew." Molly ducked her head and crawled into the tree house. "That was pretty stomach-churning."

Miri wedged herself into a corner to make room for her sister. Cookie squeaked a protest, and Miri scowled at her. "You! You practically broke my neck! I'm lucky I fell into that window over there," she explained to Molly, pointing. "I guess it's a window, anyway. Or maybe it's just where the boards have fallen off."

"Not the sturdiest tree house in the world," Molly remarked, looking through the branches. "But cute."

With guilt in the twenty-first century and war in the nineteenth, the twentieth century seemed, at first glance, like a vacation. The golden autumn afternoon was drawing to a close. In the depths of the tree, the shadows were deep and cool, but out in the branches, the leaves of the elm glittered bright, and over by the barn, comfortable animal sounds percolated. Ahead of them, the house lay clean and white and normal, looking like it had never heard of magic.

"It's so calm and peaceful, compared with the war," murmured Miri. She scratched under Cookie's ears, forgiving her. Cookie lifted a soft paw and patted her face gently.

"We don't need calm and peaceful," Molly reminded her. "We need Maudie."

It was true. They needed Maudie. They needed her to believe their story; they needed her to understand why they had to have the safe-conduct from General Lee. Then they needed her to smuggle it out of the house and let them depart with it in their hands.

A few moments later, they were standing on the wide, clean front porch, listening to someone play a piano, very badly, inside. In Miri's arms, Cookie gave a discontented huff.

Molly knocked on the door, and the response was immediate. "Shut up that playing," snipped a voice from inside. Heels thudded heavily down the hall. "There's Mr. Gardner calling, and he don't want to hear any of that racket."

Flo *again*. Miri and Molly had time only to look tragically at each other before she wrenched open the door, squealing, "Well, Mr. Gardner! Do—" The toothy smile dropped from her face and was replaced by a scowl. "You! Gypsy thieves! You can just take yourselves right off my porch. I thought I made myself clear last time you came around!"

"We're not here to see you," Miri snapped. "We're here to see your sister." On a whim, she added, "And you'd better watch out or I'll put a Gypsy curse on you."

Flo drew back. "Ain't no such thing as a curse, you nasty child!"

Miri couldn't help herself. "See what you think tomorrow morning when your eyes are scabbed shut," she said, waving her hands in a complicated pattern.

"*Stop that!*" Flo squealed.

At the sound of Flo's squeal, Cookie lurched up and scrambled for safety, jumping from Miri's arms and shooting into the hallway.

"Cookie! Come back!" Miri called after her.

"Eeeew!" squeaked Flo. "Get it, get it!"

"We can't," said Molly. "We can't go inside."

"You certainly can't," sniffed Flo. She squalled, "*Mau-DIE!* There's a cat loose in the house! Get it!"

"A cat! Really?" said a light, bubbling voice down the hall. Miri heard Molly draw in her breath. After a moment, they heard, "Oooh, come here, darling; come here, sweetheart."

"Uck!" sneered Flo.

"That's it," crooned Maudie, appearing in the hallway. Under her chin, she cuddled the white kitten. "I think this kitty's just hungry, is all—why, look!" She beamed at Miri and Molly. "It's my two favorite Gypsies! Did you come back to tell me my fortune?"

Miri thought Maudie had grown even prettier in the week since she'd seen her. "Hi," she said shyly. "Can you come outside?"

"Whyn't you come in?" urged Maudie. "I'll get you some gingerbread."

"Absolutely not!" cried Flo. "They are not putting one foot in this house. I just cleaned it."

Maudie gave her sister a steady look. "They're my company, and they can come in if they like."

"Uh. Wait," Miri said, holding up a hand to stop their argument. "We, um, can't come in. It's—it's against Gypsy rules. Will you come outside?"

Maudie's face fell. "You feel unwelcome."

"That's because they are unwelcome," put in Flo.

"No! Really, it's not that. Please come outside," Miri begged.

"Please!" added Molly, a little breathlessly.

"All right." She stepped out onto the porch with featherlight steps. The door slammed shut behind her.

Miri looked curiously at the cat in Maudie's arms. She nudged Molly. "Cookie's still here. She went inside and she's still here," she murmured. It was true. Molly gave the cat a brief, startled stare. But she didn't have time to ponder it. They needed that safe-conduct. "Maudie," Miri began.

"Take a seat," said Maudie in a friendly way. She sat down on the top step of the porch and patted the step beside her. Miri sat.

After a moment, Molly did the same.

Miri took a breath. "Maudie," she said, "I know this is going to be hard to believe, but please, just listen to me, okay?" Maudie nodded agreeably, and Miri plunged in. "We're not from here—I mean, we're not from this time."

Maudie frowned. "Pardon me?"

Miri tried again. "We're from another time, Molly and me. We live in this house a hundred years from now and—"

Maudie's face was worried. She put her hand on Miri's shoulder and whispered confidentially, "You're awful young to drink, honey. It'll stunt your growth."

"Oh gosh, Maudie, you've just got to believe us—"

"She's joking," Molly broke in suddenly. "We just have a funny way of talking about time, because we're Gypsies, and we can see into the future." She smiled into Maudie's concerned face. "Do you want to know what I see in yours?"

Maudie's cheeks flushed pink. "Oh yes!" she said, thrusting out her hand. "Tell me everything!"

Molly took Maudie's small hand in hers and ran a finger over the lines in her palm. "Well." She swallowed and looked at Miri. Help me.

"You're going to be happy," Miri said. "You're going to fall in love—"

"With who?" cried Maudie.

"A stranger," Miri answered. She looked at Molly. "Someone you don't know yet."

"You're going to meet him soon," said Molly. Her voice trembled a little. "And then you're going to marry him. You'll marry him and then you'll go to Niagara Falls on your honeymoon."

"Niagara Falls! How funny!"

Miri watched Molly, gazing into the little hand as if she truly saw the future there.

"After you've been married for a few years, you're going to have a baby."

"Ohh," Maudie sighed happily. "That's good. I love babies."

Molly's fingers curled close around her mother's. "It'll be a daughter. You'll love her and she'll love you back." Her voice fell to a whisper. "You might worry if—if—you have to leave her, but she'll be fine." She paused to take a shaking breath. "She'll find a perfect place, with a family who loves her and takes care of her, and her life will be wonderful. But she's not ever going to forget you, and—and she wants you to be happy." She gazed intently at Maudie. "So just please be as happy as you can for as long as you can. Okay?"

Maudie nodded dreamily. "A daughter," she murmured. "That's what I'd like. Maybe a boy later, but a girl first. That's just right."

Molly looked away, blinking back tears.

"Maudie," Miri began, trying to keep her voice soft and persuasive. "Last time you said that you'd pay us if we told your fortune."

"Oh, of course," exclaimed Maudie, rising. "Let me just run inside—"

"No!" Miri clutched her arm. "No, we don't want money. We need to, um, borrow something you have."

"Really? What?" Maudie looked a little wary.

"The safe-conduct signed by R. E. Lee," Miri

blurted in a rush. "Please, please. We need it for a special, uh"—she looked at Molly—"thing."

"The safe-conduct? Signed by Lee?" Maudie frowned. "That's all you want? That old piece of paper?"

Miri and Molly nodded in unison.

"You can't use it anymore," Maudie warned. "It's no good."

"We know. We still need it," Miri said.

Maudie stood, brushing off her skirt. "I'll be right back." She dropped Cookie into Molly's arms.

They waited in tense silence. "It's getting late," commented Miri. The elm was shaded by the house now, and the blue of the sky was darkening. Behind them, the sun was setting in thick stripes of gray cloud and golden light. *How many hours do they have left?* asked the voice in her mind. Miri began to chew on her knuckle.

"Here." Maudie came toward them, holding out a brown, battered sheet of paper.

Miri took it carefully in her hands and read the spindly writing. "Bearer must in no way and for no purpose be detained from the pursuit of his duties. Let neither his costume nor his demeanor cause his arrest. He is in my service. General R. E. Lee." Thank you, General R. E. Lee, she thought reverently. Whoever the heck you are.

Maudie shrugged and bent over Cookie in Molly's arms. "She's the very sweetest little thing I ever saw," she cooed.

"You want to hold her again?" Molly said, and softly transferred the kitten to Maudie. "She likes you."

At that moment, a shining motorcar rumbled onto the drive at the bottom of the yard. It came to a stop with a great grinding of gears and quivering of tires.

"Must be Flo's caller," mumbled Maudie, burying her face in Cookie's fur.

Once the engine had exhausted itself, a door slammed, and a tall, tanned man strode energetically up the lawn. "As I live and breathe, it's the Gypsy thieves!" he called cheerfully, waving.

Maudie looked up, startled, and Cookie, seized by a sense of drama, leaped from her arms to streak white across the lawn.

"Oh, goodness!" cried Maudie, laughing. "Can you catch her?"

Pat Gardner grinned. "I don't have very good luck with this cat." But obligingly he leaned down and, by some strange chance, scooped Cookie into his hands. "Or maybe I do."

"Thanks!" said Maudie, hurrying down the stairs to retrieve the kitten.

Pat straightened, and Miri and Molly, standing on the top step, saw his face as the girl came toward him. They saw his smile grow still and his eyes widen.

"Look. She's wearing a yellow dress," whispered Molly.

She was. Miri hadn't noticed it before, but in the glowing sunset, Maudie skimming across the grass looked like light itself.

Fumbling a little, Pat Gardner handed the kitten to Maudie. For a moment, the pair of them stood, looking at each other.

"You see?" said a voice behind them. As Miri spun around, Molly was already hurtling into May's arms.

"Oh, Grandma," she cried, nestling her head in her grandmother's shoulder. "Is it all right? I could've stopped them, and I didn't. I didn't do anything!"

May's arms circled Molly and rocked her gently. "Look at them, sweetheart. Look!" she commanded, and turned Molly around to watch as Maudie, blushing now, tried to hold Cookie and shake hands with Pat at the same time. Every movement between them was both awkward and the most graceful thing Miri had ever seen. "Look. They've finally met. And they're about to fall in love," May said in a low voice. "Without you, it would never have happened. Flo would have seen to that. And sweetheart," she said, stroking Molly's hair, "it would have been a sin to stop it. This is what Maudie would choose. If she had to choose between six years with Pat Gardner and a long life without him, she would choose him."

"Really?" asked Molly anxiously.

"I've seen her make the choice before." May's bright jewel eyes smiled at Molly. "You've given her what she wants most. Pat Gardner and you."

"What about the rest of it?" Miri begged. "Are we going to save Ray and Robbie?"

May's face went blank. "There is never only one way the story can turn out."

Miri's stomach flopped. "So it depends on us."

There was a moment of silence. "If you . . . don't

succeed," said May, "the boys will not have existed in your lives. Your mother and father won't feel it. No one will feel it."

"Except us," said Miri miserably.

May nodded, her brilliant eyes tender.

"It's all our fault," Miri mourned. "If we hadn't interfered with Jamie and his uncle, Ray and Robbie wouldn't have been caught by Carter."

"You mustn't despair, child. Time is so very, very complicated that it's impossible to know if you have changed the story or made it what it was supposed to be. Impossible. But"—May closed her eyes—"in any version of the story, you did right for Jamie. His survival is important, not just to him"—her eyes flew open, and she smiled—"but to some others as well." Gently, she took her arms away from Molly. "I think it's time now, sweetheart."

Molly nodded without speaking, and the two girls turned toward the door of the house.

"Wait," said Miri, stopping midstep. "We don't have Cookie."

"Leave her," said May. "Leave her for now." She lifted her eyes to the scene on the lawn. "Her job isn't done."

Miri began to protest, but Molly interrupted. "She'll come to visit us, won't she?"

May smiled. "Of course. You'll see her all the time. All the times."

The girls turned for one final look at Maudie and Pat, petting Cookie between them. "Bye," whispered Molly.

❖ CHAPTER ❖

15

MOLLY PAUSED, a carton of eggs in her hands. "They looked happy, didn't they?"

"Really happy," Miri confirmed, dumping a pile of energy bars on the kitchen table. "You think eight bars is enough?"

"Yeah. Eight," said Molly. She smiled. "It was love at first sight for him, don't you think?"

"Totally," said Miri. She glanced over the contents of their basket: flashlight, to get them through the woods; eggs, to get them into the Colonel's presence; Band-Aids, for Robbie's head; energy bars, because their brothers were always starving; and most precious of all, the safe-conduct, the slim, battered piece of paper that was their only chance against the stupidity of war.

It has to work, Miri said to herself.

There is never only one way the story can turn out.

Molly looked toward the darkening window. "Let's get going."

"I need to change into a dress," Miri said.

Molly, already wearing a dress, nodded impatiently. "Hurry."

Miri sped toward the stairs. But in the hallway, she stopped suddenly and made an abrupt turn into her mother's office. There, she clicked on the lamp, revealing a room thick with papers. Papers slid from baskets and off the mountaintops of other papers. Stapled papers met unstapled papers and merged with folders, catalogs, books, letters, and scraps to make vast seas of papers. Miri looked at the mess, trying to think like her mother. Oh. She turned to the bookshelf, to a box labeled HOUSE. She lifted the lid and found herself looking at the yellowed newspaper ad for F. Gibbons's dining room table and coffin. Quickly, she lifted it and found the scowling woman, the lace-swaddled baby, and—what she was looking for. She peered intently at the picture of the two laughing soldiers. Could it be? Their chins were identical. But their hair wasn't. It looked like one had dark hair. But maybe it was a shadow.

And the smiles, the way they were holding in their laughs and not succeeding. It could be them. It could also be any pair of teenage brothers. But it *could* be them. It could be Robbie and Ray, unharmed. In the 1860s, in the war, but unhanged and unharmed. Not her brothers anymore, lost to her forever. But not killed. Maybe.

She just couldn't tell. Because the photo was too dark, the brothers too hidden. And because there was never only one way the story could turn out.

She threw the picture back into the box and hurried from the room.

She wanted her brothers. That was the ending she wanted.

. . .

In both of their previous trips, the empty silence that hung over the land had given Miri the creeps, but after fifteen minutes in the woods, she longed for it. The dusky gloom was punctuated by unexplainable noises: sudden pops and cracks, soft scurries and breaths. Things approached, stopped short, and were heard scrambling away. Once or twice, far-off voices seemed to call out. Miri's ears ached to turn the sounds into something known; a shushing in the distance, and her mind said: car on the road. But there was no road, no car, and some very old part of her knew she was hearing something hunting something else. She longed to run.

They were moving as fast as they could, but no one would call it running. They couldn't see more than a few feet ahead, so it was more like hopping. And often, they hopped wrong. "Uck!" Miri detached cobwebs from her face. "Let's use the flashlight," she said. "We might never make it there if we don't."

Molly flicked it on, and immediately, there was a startled headlong rush in the bushes next to them. Heavy footsteps crashed away through the darkness. When the noise died away, the two girls found themselves wrapped in each other's arms.

"He was right beside us!" chattered Miri. "Was he following us?"

"I don't know. Probably not. Probably he was just hiding and we scared him." Molly gave a long shudder. She snapped the flashlight off, and they resumed their hesitant journey.

"I guess in a war, there are lots of people trying not to get caught," said Miri. "Northern guys,

Southern guys, people who don't want to fight, people who do want to fight—" She was interrupted by a distant sobbing yowl.

"Animals," added Molly.

Miri paused, her ears tingling as they searched for information. "I don't think that was an animal."

. . .

After what felt like hours, there was a light in the distance. Then two. Then several, shining in different spots, different brightnesses. Compared with the woods, Paxton looked like New York City, and Miri had never been so glad to see it. She and Molly burst from the dark canopy of trees, ducking from the shelter of one small structure to another until they were at the same jutting white corner they had peeked around that afternoon.

The scrubby lawn was empty. Though they hadn't really expected the boys to be sitting there still, Miri and Molly searched anxiously for clues, signs, evidence of their whereabouts. Nothing. Nothing but trees. Where were they? Had they been taken somewhere for safekeeping? Or—Miri didn't want to think it, but she did—had the Colonel grown impatient? Were they too late?

Miri heard Molly swallow hard. "I know," Miri said, trying to sound calm and reasonable. "But I bet they're fine! I'm almost sure they are! They're probably locked up somewhere, safe and sound. No problem. We'll just go and show the pass to the Colonel ourselves. We can say they gave it to us. And hey, look!" She pointed at the porch. "The guard is gone! We can bust right in and find the Colonel, easy-peasy." *Easy-peasy?* sneered her brain. Who are you kidding?

As they crossed the porch, Molly whispered, "Remember to look like an innocent little—" A sudden whoop from within the house drowned out her voice.

What kind of person has a party in the middle of a war? thought Miri indignantly. The Colonel, apparently. At the end of the murky entryway stood a bright doorway, streaming light, laughter, shouts, and the clatter of dishes. Bits of conversation, calls to pass the beans, and the thump of boots against floor came from within.

"Innocent little girls," repeated Molly, "with eggs for the Colonel's breakfast." She lifted the basket with eggs nestled in Easter grass.

"Innocent little girls with eggs for the Colonel's

breakfast," confirmed Miri. They tucked the egg carton, together with the energy bars, the Band-Aids, and all other signs of the twenty-first century under a chest of drawers. They turned for one final inspection in the enormous hall mirror.

"Smile!" whispered Molly.

Two innocent little girls with huge smiles plastered on their faces tiptoed down the hall and peeked through the doorway. It was a big room, a dining room, Miri supposed. There was a long table, lined with men—not a woman in sight—and they were all yelling. Miri couldn't understand what they were yelling *about*, exactly. Some of them seemed to be singing, some of them seemed to be chewing, some of them seemed to be arguing, and some of them seemed to be singing, chewing, and arguing all at the same time. No one noticed the two innocent little girls in the doorway. Searching for the Colonel, Miri's eyes zipped from face to face—there was Hern, glugging a drink, but Carter did not seem to have been invited. He probably wasn't very popular, she thought.

"Con-*fusion* to the em-en-em," hollered Hern suddenly, slapping his hand on the table. "Con-*fusion* to the em-emily!"

"To the enemy!" corrected a nearby soldier.

A bellow of agreement rose from one end of the table, followed by much slamming of cups.

Where was the Colonel? Had he gone to fight a battle? In the dark? Miri and Molly exchanged worried glances.

There was a burst of song: *"God SAVE the SOUTH! God SAVE the South!"*

"Her AAAAL-ters and FIIIIIRE-sides!"

"GOD SAVE THE SOUTH!" they wailed in unison.

A heavy soldier rose unsteadily to his feet—it was the guard from the porch, very pink. *"Gentlemen!"* he cried. *"Gentlemen! Let us not neglect the first duty of a Ranger."* He raised his glass so energetically that it flew out of his fingers and shattered against the wall. He looked at his hand in surprise. "Where'd it go?"

Another soldier popped up, glass ready. "I give you . . . the Colonel!"

Cheers and whistles. "The *Colonel*!!"

"If you boys would pipe down, Colonel might could get a little sleep," grumbled a soldier with an enormous black mustache. "Poor feller would rather sleep than listen to y'all's shindy, I bet."

Aha! The Colonel was asleep! Upstairs, probably. In what the hoopskirt tour-guide ladies had called the "elegant Buckley bedchambers." The girls withdrew from the doorway and slipped up the stairs. Behind them, another glass shattered.

At the top of the stairs, they paused uncertainly. Seven closed doors lined the hallway. The Colonel was behind one of them. But which one?

Not the farthest one, at the end of the hall. He was too important to sleep at the back of the house. He'd be in one of the rooms near the front, almost for sure. Miri pointed at the three doors ahead. Molly nodded agreement. He'd be in one of these. But which one? There were two doors on one side of the hall; one door on the other.

The single door had to lead to the largest room. The largest room had to be the Colonel's. He was, after all, the leader of his troops. Plus Mrs. Hibbs had a crush on him. Surely she'd give him the biggest room.

Again, Miri pointed, at the lone door. Again, Molly nodded. Carefully, silently, they approached it. Molly grasped the knob and slowly began to turn it. Miri held her breath, wincing, waiting for a squeak or a squeal to betray them.

But the door opened without a sound, and they

whisked inside. The room was large—and dark, lit only by the moonlight streaming in the window. Miri could see, in the moon-glow, a shining wooden dresser and the china bowl and pitcher that the Buckleys washed their faces in. But most of the space was occupied by a gigantic canopy bed ("Imported from France!" the hoopskirt ladies had gushed). And in the bed—Miri pointed again—lay a sleeping figure. Molly nodded. They tiptoed to the bedside and looked at the unmoving lump of the Colonel.

Miri cleared her throat softly. The Colonel didn't budge.

Miri cleared her throat a little less softly.

Nothing.

"Sir?" Molly whispered.

The Colonel lay still as death.

Hoping he wasn't the grumpy-waking-up type, Miri reached out and gently shook his shoulder. "Sir," she murmured. "Sir."

A quick scratch, a flame bursting into light, and Miri found herself looking straight into two yellow eyes.

For a split second, she froze. Then—

Carter's hand closed around her arm.

⤙ CHAPTER ⤚

16

"LET GO," said Miri, but her voice was quaking. She could hear it, and so could Carter.

"Stop sniveling," he sneered, tightening his fingers on her arm. "You made a fool of me yesterday, girl. It's not an experience I enjoy, being humiliated. I find it upsetting. It upsets me." He smiled slowly. "I am therefore charmed by your unexpected reappearance."

She kicked at his knee, but he had learned that trick the day before, and he simply held her farther away, shaking his head. "You insult me." He looked up at Molly, still smiling. "You brats need to learn a lesson. And I shall be your teacher."

Molly sneered at him. "You insult me," she said,

and then she opened her mouth and screamed, high, piercing, and long.

At once, there was a thump and a rattle in the hallway, and light flooded in as the door flew open. "What's the matter? What the devil's the matter?" cried the Colonel, his face white above a candle.

Carter flung Miri away from him. "Assassins!" he exclaimed. "These devils crept in thinking it was your bed, sir, and put a knife to my throat."

"Not true!" yelled Miri, but she was drowned out by a stampede of boots on the stairs.

"Sir! Sir!" cried a jumble of voices. "Colonel! Save the Colonel! We'll get 'em! You all right? Sir?" Men thronged into the room, pistols waving wildly as they bellowed and crashed into one another.

"Stand down!" roared someone. "Stand down, you fools!" Miri saw that it was the grumbling soldier from the dining room. He was shorter and younger than most of the others, but they obeyed him, subsiding into confused silence, their pistols dropping to their sides, their feet shuffling.

"Thank you, Charlie," said the Colonel. "And thank you, gentlemen, for your, uh, enthusiastic defense of my person. As you can see, I am in no immediate danger of annihilation." His smile flashed. "Unlike some of you, who appear to be in the last stages of a consumption of spirituous liquors. You are dismissed. Return to your debauches. Except you, Charlie, and Carter. And our guests, of course." He bowed slightly toward Miri and Molly.

"Don't be fooled by their size, Colonel," warned Carter as the other soldiers bumbled away. "They're out for your neck, that's certain. Someone's sold you out, sir, and these cubs were aiming to get the bounty on your head." His pale eyes gleamed with concern, and Miri felt a stab of envy for his ability to lie convincingly. In less than a minute, he'd managed to turn himself into the Colonel's faithful rescuer.

Now the Colonel turned to inspect Miri and Molly. His face gave no hint of his opinion.

"No, sir, no," Miri began. "We're not doing anything like that, sir—"

"Then explain," snapped Carter, "what, precisely, you *were* about, slinking through bedrooms in the dark."

The Colonel glanced at the basket that still hung, in spite of everything, over Molly's arm and said quietly, "I'd advise you not to say eggs."

"No, of course not! We only brought the eggs to keep Mrs. Hibbs from fussing," Molly said quickly.

The Colonel nodded and looked at Miri. "Explain yourself, if you please."

Miri's heart began to thunder in her chest. "We came about—about—about some prisoners. Two boys he"—she pointed at Carter—"caught and beat up today." What if he didn't believe them? What if he didn't listen? He *had* to.

The Colonel lifted his eyebrows inquiringly at Carter.

Carter frowned at Miri, trying to figure out what she was up to, before he turned to the Colonel. "The two prisoners I told you about. Yankees. Emory's." He shrugged. "Captured to fill the order for tomorrow."

"We saw them, today, this afternoon, when we came here," Miri said, "and when the guard told us that they were going to—to—to"—she took a breath—"be hanged tomorrow, we thought we should say a prayer with them—for them to get into heaven, you know?" She nodded hopefully at the Colonel. Maybe he was religious.

He rolled his eyes. "A charming sentiment. They're enemy combatants."

Not religious. Molly cut in, "And while we were praying with them, they said we should give you a message. They said *he*"—she looked at Carter— "would never believe it, but you would. It's a letter." The small brown paper trembled as she held it out.

The Colonel looked at it, bored. "Let me guess. They're the sole support of an ancient mother."

"And a one-legged sister," laughed the soldier named Charlie. Miri and Molly looked at each other in dismay. It had never occurred to them that the Colonel would refuse to read the letter.

Carter broke in, "Sir, let me take care of these children for you. I'll teach them a thing or two, and then I'll return them to their loving families. Please," he begged. "I'm so fond of the kiddies." He laid a heavy hand on Miri's shoulder.

Miri shuddered and ducked away.

"Colonel, I know you don't believe us, but please read it," Molly implored. "It's important. *Please*. You'll see."

The Colonel sighed. "More light, please."

Carter snapped a match between his fingers and lit the candle beside the bed.

Charlie snorted. "Fire's the devil's friend, eh, Nick?" He lit another candle from Carter's flame.

The Colonel unfolded the paper and tilted it toward the candlelight. Breathlessly, Miri watched his eyes race over the words, stop, and go back to the beginning, reading slowly. A moment later, he lifted his head and gave Carter a sharp look. "Get those boys. Bring them here at once. No!" He spun around to Charlie. "You get them."

Success! thought Miri, darting a wild glance at Molly. But one look at Carter's face drove her triumph away. He was watching her, his yellow eyes flat, one eyebrow raised, his teeth slowly moving, one row against another, from side to side. He caught her watching him and smiled. "How I love the kiddies," he murmured, and Miri felt the skin on the back of her neck crawl.

The Colonel said nothing. For what seemed like years, they stood in silence. If only I could call a time-out, Miri thought, shifting her weight from foot to foot. If only I could say, Excuse me, sir, Molly and I need to go into the hall for a minute. If only we could communicate telepathically. If only—she looked up to find Molly's clear gray eyes fixed on her, and for a moment, she relaxed. Molly knew what to do, Miri could tell. Molly knew they had to start talking, loud, about the safe-conduct the moment their brothers came through the door. Molly got it. Miri gave her a tiny nod, and Molly nodded in return.

Wow, thought Miri. Maybe that *was* telepathic communication.

But what about Ray and Robbie? They had no idea what they were facing, what role they were supposed to play. No warning, no preparation. And they're such dopes, Miri thought despairingly, they'll never catch on. Plus, they're crappy improvisers. Her stomach lurched as she remembered Ray protesting that he'd only cut history once. They were terrible at faking it even when they knew what they were supposed to be faking. This was going to be a disaster.

Nervously, Miri put her knuckle in her mouth, decided that knuckle-chewing looked suspicious, removed it, clasped her hands together, decided that looked suspicious, too, unclasped them, threw herself on the mercy of the gods and prayed that her brothers would be granted intelligence, just for the next twenty minutes, please please please. Don't let them say that we're their sisters. Don't let them blab about reenactments. Don't let them be stupid, she begged. And especially don't let them be so stupid as to say they have no idea who R. E. Lee is and they've never seen the safe-conduct before in their lives. Miri panicked. They were that stupid. She groaned quietly.

"Are you unwell?" asked the Colonel.

"No! No!" Miri assured him. "I'm just fine. Just great. A-okay!"

Molly rolled her eyes: shut up.

Miri shut up. Think of something else, she urged herself. She looked around the room hopefully. The elegant Buckley bedchamber smelled a little funky. Like pee. There were no bathrooms, she remembered. Just chamber pots. Yuck. And the Colonel and Carter both seemed to sleep in their clothes. No wonder they smelled. Everyone in the twenty-first century complained about pollution, but they'd never gotten a whiff of the nineteenth—

Her thoughts were disrupted by thumps, turning into footsteps on the stairs. "Pick up your feet, boy," said Charlie's voice outside the door. There was a pause and a knock. "Colonel."

"Enter."

The door swung open, and Ray and Robbie shuffled in, herded by Charlie. In the split second before they saw her, Miri inspected them—Robbie's face was still bloodstained, and the gash where the gun barrel had cut him was still open. A blue-and-brown bruise had spread over his forehead since she'd seen him last. But he seemed to be more awake, not as dopey; his eyes were scanning the room, seeking information. She saw him flinch at the sight of Carter. And then he saw her and Molly.

There was one second for all four of them to exchange looks, and in that second, Miri thought with all her might, Be smart.

"Sir!" Molly began. "The—

But the Colonel silenced her with an upraised hand. "I am leading this investigation, if you please." Molly's mouth shut with a snap of frustration, and the Colonel turned to Robbie. "How'd you get that, soldier?" he asked, nodding at his forehead.

Robbie looked at Carter. "Him."

The Colonel lifted an eyebrow at Carter, who shrugged. "Accident of capture. He resisted."

"Ah," said the Colonel. He turned back to Robbie. "Did you attempt to explain your situation to Private Carter here?"

"Well, sure!" Ray exclaimed. "We tried to tell him, but he just hauled off and slammed Robbie in the face with his gun!"

"They told me nothing!" growled Carter.

"That's 'cause he couldn't talk after you'd hit him!" said Miri loudly.

Carter lifted a disdainful eyebrow. "You weren't there."

"Yes, we were," said Molly unexpectedly. She smiled her innocent-little-girl smile at the Colonel. "Me and my sister were walking in our field and saw the whole thing—Mr. Carter here, he just lifted up his gun and smacked that boy upside the head, for no reason at all that we could see! It was terrible! And then he made them march, even though the poor thing was bleeding like a stuck pig." She shook her head sadly. "We never saw such a dreadful sight in our lives, so we followed along, hoping to minister to the wounded."

"Wait, you guys were there, too?" Ray said.

Miri rushed to drown him out: "That's why we came here this afternoon. The eggs were just a—a—an alibi!" Did they use that word during the Civil War? She hoped so. On she galloped: "And then your guard said they were going to get hanged, so we prayed with them, and that's when they showed us their *safe-conduct from General Lee*!" she said it as loudly as she dared. "Their *pass*." Listen, she begged Ray and Robbie silently. Pay attention, for once in your lives.

The room fell silent as the Colonel looked from the paper in his hand to Robbie and Ray, to Carter, to Miri and Molly, and finally, back to the paper.

"Lies," said Carter softly. The Colonel lifted his head. "Nonsense. Bunkum. Do you really suppose, sir, that General Lee would endow such"—he flicked a contemptuous finger at the boys—"such tadpoles with any serious responsibility? Preposterous! They're Yankees, scouts for some more accomplished villain, no doubt, who intends to slit your throat while you sleep, sir. This story," he sneered at Miri, "is mush, peddled by children who wish to make themselves important. Surely, sir, you would not be deceived by such a falsehood." He curled his eyebrow. "If you will take my advice, sir, you'll let me take care of these brats, put the Yankees back in the stable, and shoot them at first light tomorrow. Like Custer shot our boys."

"They do seem a mite green," murmured the Colonel.

"Right!" agreed Molly. "Way too young to die."

"I meant they seem a mite green to be in the general's service," the Colonel said. "How old are you boys?"

"Thirteen," answered Robbie with infuriating honesty.

The Colonel frowned.

"Bah," said Carter. "He's sixteen if he's a day, and he's lying for all he's worth. Bald-faced prevarication and perjury. Trying to save his own skin. He's a Yankee soldier, and I say we kill him." His yellow eyes glittered. He was winning.

"'Let neither *his costume nor his demeanor* cause his arrest,'" quoted Miri loudly. "'He is in my service.'"

The Colonel nodded, true.

"*He*," drawled Carter. "Singular. If this missive were truly from General Lee, which it is not, would it not make reference to two boys? After all, there *are* two boys here."

"That's so." The Colonel nodded.

Miri looked helplessly at Molly. What were they to do? But Molly's eyes only reflected her own desperation.

And then Ray spoke. "Hello? Look at us. We're identical," he said casually. "That's the whole point."

Miri saw Robbie's eyes flicker to Ray's. Then he said, "Yeah. We're interchangeable. That's why he picked us. Even if we are thirteen."

Miri stared at them in astonishment. They were brilliant.

"That doesn't explain a thing!" cried Carter. "There's still two of them and one pass!"

Ray looked at him calmly. "One of us is supposed to get caught. And then—well, that's the secret part. And you know, pal, we're actually supposed to be somewhere else right now."

"Yeah," Robbie said, shaking his head. "The general is not going to be happy about this." He pointed to the gash on his head. "Or this. Now they can tell the difference between us."

"What a screwup," Ray sighed.

"Not our fault," Robbie said. He jerked his head in Carter's direction. "His fault."

Carter looked uneasily between them. "Nonsense. Lies."

There was a pause. Miri held her breath.

The Colonel plucked at his shirt collar for a few moments, finally bursting out, "I do wish you'd managed to keep those prisoners alive yesterday,

Carter. If they hadn't died in your care, I'd never have needed replacements. And it looks like you've caused us a peck of trouble in finding them. I'll write my apologies to General Lee, but you've made a serious blunder and dishonored all of us by it."

He believed them! The four children exchanged lightning-quick glances of joy.

Carter tried to regain his lost advantage. "Now, sir," he said with a wink, "wouldn't you say it's something of a stretcher, these small fry playing a big game for the Command? Look at 'em—"

"Silence! It's not for you to question the workings of your betters," snapped the Colonel. He turned to the boys, and Miri gave a small, involuntary bounce on her toes as he handed the safe-conduct to Ray. They'd done it! They were safe! They were free! But the Colonel was speaking, "Please accept my apologies and proceed under your orders from General Lee. I'll write to him at once to explain the cause"—he glared at Carter—"of your tardiness."

"Okay," said Ray. Robbie inclined his head graciously.

"And you, young ladies," said the Colonel,

nodding to Molly and Miri, "your service to the Cause will not go unnoticed in my letter. Accept the humble thanks of the Confederacy for your swift and loyal action."

Eww. Miri didn't want to accept the thanks of the Confederacy. The Confederacy stank. They were the bad guys. The slave owners. Boo! She was tempted to yell something like "Long Live the United States!" or "Hooray for Abraham Lincoln!" Maybe she should start singing "The Star-Spangled Banner." But she couldn't. They'd lose everything they'd just won, including Robbie and Ray. No, she had to be strategic and mature and controlled. It was hard. It felt wrong. Shouldn't she do something for the side of right and justice? Here she was, in the middle of the Civil War, a time-traveler! She should do something good and brave and wonderful and patriotic. Wasn't magic for setting things right?

Ray and Robbie gave the Colonel something that looked vaguely like a salute. "So long!" said Ray.

The Colonel nodded, dismissing them.

Molly renewed her innocent-little-girl smile. "I guess we'll be going now," she said, taking a step toward the door.

Miri stood frozen where she was. If she didn't do something good and brave and patriotic, she didn't deserve to have magic happen to her.

"I guess we'll be *going* now," Molly repeated, looking at her sister.

It would be setting something right, no doubt about that. It might save someone's life.

"Miri!" whispered Molly.

Miri ignored her. "Sir," she said. The Colonel raised his eyes. "Sir, you should know, the prisoners yesterday didn't die." She didn't dare look at Carter as she said it. She'd get too scared. "We saw it all. Carter let them go in exchange for three hundred dollars in gold." She left Hern out of it. He'd saved her life. Or at least not ended it. "Those men you fought yesterday were guards. Railroad guards. The two wounded guys had a lot of money, in gold, and Carter took it and let them go. I bet he's got it hidden here somewhere." Miri waved her hand at the room.

"Colonel!" Carter exploded. "This wretched brat has gone too far—"

But the Colonel cut him off. "Charlie."

"Yessir." Charlie, Miri saw, had eased a pistol

out of some pocket or other and was now pointing it at Carter. "Just you hold still, Nick," he advised. As his eyes circled the bedroom, he began to speak softly, "And now's when you ask yourself, if I was Nick Carter, where'd I hide gold eagles? And you answer yourself pretty easy, 'cause Nick Carter, he don't just think he's smart." Charlie moved toward the dresser. "Nick thinks everyone else is dumb." He reached for a small chest sitting atop the dresser and flipped it open. "If he had any sense, he'd a hid it," he said calmly. "But Nick here is so smart he's stupid." Charlie pulled a leather pouch from the chest. "He thinks no one but him has any brains atall. Especially if they don't talk fancy." He shook the pouch open with one hand, and ten gold coins rolled out. "Aw, Nick. You'd sell your own mother, wouldn't you? There's a hundred." He picked one up and looked at it carefully. "United States of America. 1864. Eagle." He flipped it at the Colonel, who caught it easily and inspected it.

"That proves nothing!" gasped Carter. "Lies! All of it! I won those eagles, fair and square, in a game of chance! This was no prisoner's gold! The girl is in the pay of the enemy, don't you see it? She's lying through her teeth, devil take her, and I'll—"

"Quiet!" roared the Colonel. It was the loudest sound Miri had ever heard him make, and it silenced the room. There was a long pause. Finally, the Colonel spoke: "Once again, and for the last time, you've gone too far." He glared bitterly at Carter. "As if it weren't enough, fighting Northerners. Is it too much to ask that you should not make war on your own country? No, it's insupportable. You are herewith discharged from the Forty-Third Virginia Cavalry. Dishonorably."

Carter's face flushed dark. "Sir, you can't do that—"

The Colonel cut him off. "You shall take the place of your prisoners, Carter. Count yourself lucky that I don't require you to take their place in the noose tomorrow morning."

Carter drew himself up. "You do me an insult I will not bear—"

There was a click that Miri realized came from Charlie's pistol.

"Charlie, please accompany Carter to the brig. Tell Williams, with my compliments, that I present him with a prisoner to replace the two I took."

Carter stared at the Colonel in disbelief. "How can this be? I'm to be ruined on the word of a child?"

"Looks like it!" called Miri gleefully.

"Boom-roasted!" agreed Ray.

The Colonel reproved them with a look and turned to Carter. "Out of the mouths of babes hast thou ordained strength, that thou might still the enemy and the avenger," he recited.

Carter glared furiously at the children and stalked out the door. Charlie followed him, an enormous grin under his black mustache.

Silence fell over the room. Miri could hear a clock ticking in the hallway. After a moment, Molly set the basket of eggs on the rug. "You can have the eggs," she whispered.

The Colonel sighed. "Thank you, miss." He glanced down at his hand. "Never let it be said that the Rangers plunder the honest citizens of Virginia." He held out the gold coin. "Payment for ten eggs."

Molly took it. "Thank you."

"The pleasure is mine." He ran his hand through his thin hair. "Dismissed."

The four children backed quickly out of the room, trying not to run. In the gloomy hall, they raced for the stairs—what if he changed his mind?—and scuttled down, slipping past the roomful of now-sleepy soldiers, scooping up the energy bars, and decamping as quickly as they could. Only when they reached the lawn, pale in the moonlight, did they allow themselves to pause and stare at one another in amazement.

At last, Molly spoke. "I can't believe you guys."

"You were incredible," Miri said. "You were geniuses."

"Yeah." Ray nodded.

"How'd you figure out what was going on?" asked Molly. "About the safe-conduct and everything."

They gave her blank looks. "We just did."

"And then the thing about how being identical was part of the plan." Miri turned to Robbie. "It was like you were reading Ray's mind."

He shrugged.

"Were you?" she pressed.

Her brothers' eyes met and veered apart. "None of your beeswax," said Robbie.

Ray looked at the energy bars in Molly's hand. "Gimme some of those."

"Why didn't you bring more?" demanded Robbie. "I'm, like, about to die of starvation."

Miri and Molly rolled their eyes. So much for

geniuses. Back to their regularly scheduled brothers. "At least you're not dying of hanging," Molly reminded them.

Neither brother replied, but as they walked across the moonlit grass, Miri felt Ray's hand pat her lightly on the head. And while he was shoving her to get another energy bar from her pocket, Robbie squeezed her arm. "What?" she asked, looking up.

"You know," he muttered.

"I know what?"

"You know, thanks."

She reached out to hug him. "Ew, girl cooties," he said, batting her away.

❖ CHAPTER ❖

17

ON THE DIRT ROAD leading away from Paxton, the four children tried to walk in a purposeful, soldier-like way, but the boys, loopy with freedom, dizzy with relief, and restored by energy bars, soon began to run. "Let's get *out of here*!" urged Ray, galloping forward. "This place gives me the heebie-jeebies."

"No!" Molly called. "Stop it! You've got to act military. Disciplined and serious."

They groaned, but they also stopped running. Robbie straightened, glanced at Molly, and tried to match his pace with hers. Ray fell into step beside Miri. "Okay," he said. "We'll be disciplined and serious, but you've got to tell us what the heck is going on here."

So they did. They told about the house and the window and the battle and Jamie and his uncle and Carter and the gold. They talked for so long and the boys asked so many questions that they were halfway through the woods by the time they were finished.

"But wait. I don't get who's in charge," said Robbie, interrupting for approximately the twentieth time. "I thought it was the Colonel."

"The Colonel's in charge of his regiment or battalion or whatever it is," Molly explained, "but General Lee is his boss. General Lee's in charge of the whole Confederate army."

"So they're bad guys?" Ray asked. "The Colonel's a bad guy?"

"Of course he is!" Molly said. "He's fighting for the South, isn't he? They're for slavery."

"But the Colonel seemed okay. And that guy Charlie didn't like Carter any better than we did." Ray frowned, confused.

Miri stopped in her tracks. "The Colonel was the one who wanted to hang you, not Carter," she reminded him. "But he's not *bad*. Just 'cause they're fighting for something bad doesn't mean *they're* bad. Not all of them and not about everything. They're just people."

The boys contemplated this. "Huh," Robbie grunted.

Ray spoke up. "Where'd you get the safe-conduct?"

Miri glanced at Molly. "We know someone who had it. She gave it to us." The boys couldn't know everything, and most especially they couldn't know the secret of Molly's past.

To change the subject, Molly leaped atop a rock. "You know, you guys have to give us anything we want, forever, because we saved your lives!"

The day before, Ray would have argued, pushed her off the rock, declared himself king. But now, he just smiled. "I can deal with that."

"Yep," Robbie agreed. And they walked on.

The woods had lost their creepiness. The creaks and sighs of the earlier journey were gone—or drowned out by the boys—and now that the moon had risen, its blue light gleamed occasionally between branches. Every once in a while, Miri's hair snagged on a leaf, but it didn't hurt much. She'd stop to uncoil it and gaze at the silvery glints of the creek. They had done it, she thought proudly. Ray and Robbie weren't going to get hanged in the morning. Molly was still in the Gill family. Maudie and Pat Gardner were in love. And Carter was in jail, chained to a boulder, she hoped. He wouldn't be able to shoot anyone, beat anyone up, or steal from anyone for a good, long time. I did that, Miri congratulated herself.

She dawdled a little on the dark path, thinking about magic, thinking about her place in it. Maybe she wasn't as quick-thinking as Molly, or as practical, but she'd done all right. And, she reminded herself, her drifting mind had actually been useful. She had drifted her way into remembering Flo and the safe-conduct, for instance. . . .

"Miri! Hurry up!" came Molly's voice from somewhere ahead.

"Wait! Wait for me!" she yelled, bursting into a run.

And there they were, Robbie, Ray, and Molly, lined up at the edge of what would be, a hundred and fifty years later, the far corner of their front yard. Up ahead, the small, mangled silhouette of the house was black against the blue night sky. A few crickety chirps sounded.

Robbie peered at the house. "What happened to it?"

"It got shelled," Molly said. "And it's smaller. But the door's the same, and that's the part we need."

"We did it," said Miri thankfully. "We're home."

Ray grinned at her in the pale moonlight. "Last one there—"

"Is a goober-butt!" sang Robbie, shooting off through the grass.

Miri dashed forward—home, home, home—but of course, they were all faster than she was. She didn't care—home, home, home—Molly and her brothers were already on the porch waiting for her. They weren't even calling her a loser for being last. That's nice of them, she thought, racing to the stairs. We'll all go in and face Mom together. Whatever the punishment is, at least we'll be together and—

"And here I was beginning to think I'd never see you again!"

In the shadows of the front porch, a figure was reclining against the door, long legs stretched out before him.

"The last little duckling makes an arrival, returning home after a long day of dispensing justice. Tired but happy."

It was Carter.

"No," Miri said, frozen at the bottom of the stairs.

"Oh yes. It's me," he said. "Restored to liberty. Risen from the tomb."

"But you're in jail," said Miri blankly. This couldn't be. The magic wouldn't allow it. They had done everything they were supposed to do. Robbie and Ray. Molly. Maudie and Pat. They had set things right. Carter wasn't *allowed* to ruin what they'd done. "I saw Charlie take you away."

"Charlie's a fool," Carter said, rising to his feet in one smooth movement. "But he's not such a fool that he's going to die if he doesn't have to. And he was generous enough to provide me—after some persuasion—with a horse and his very own pistol. Loaded." He lifted it until she could see it glinting in the moonlight. "Get up here."

Miri's heart began to thump in her chest. She joined Molly and her brothers on the porch.

"So you're going to shoot us?" said Ray after a minute.

"Yes, you *nit*, I'm going to shoot you," hissed Carter. "But not quite yet. Eventually. It took you grubs a long time to get here, and I had plentiful leisure to imagine your lingering and painful ends. I have great plans for each of you. . . ."

He talked on, but Miri stopped listening. Her heart was pounding in her throat. My poor heart, she thought sympathetically. It's had a hard day. A hard week. I've been scared so many times this past week. I'm tired of being scared.

She watched Carter's mouth move. Something about how she had tarnished his honor. Whatever. Her mind was drifting—which, she told herself, was not a bad idea under the circumstances. She wished her body could follow. She would drift through the front door.

". . . maggots, gorging on the corpse of the Carter name . . ."

What was he gabbing about? She didn't know, so she looked, instead, at his narrow yellow eyes. She'd never seen anyone with yellow eyes before. Like a cat. She wondered if he could see in the dark.

". . . and you dared to play the innocent—you!" he went on angrily. "You, a spying mudsill, and to have my reputation fouled by the likes of such a—"

With calm surprise, Miri realized that she was not actually feeling fear. Her fear seemed to have moved a few feet away from her. Maybe she had been so frightened for so long that she was hardened to it. She felt light and free. Can't scare me, she said silently to Carter, even if you are about to shoot me. She glanced over her shoulder at Molly and Ray and Robbie and hoped that fear had left them, too.

Carter bent over her, his face twisted with anger. ". . . and you will be the last to go, you devil, because I'll have you see the damage your wicked tongue has wrought."

He hates me so much, he's gone a little crazy, she thought, watching him. His face in the moonlight looked dark, almost purple, and little pieces of spit flew from his mouth as he thundered at her. He hates me so much he can't even think, she realized. He can't concentrate on anything but hating me.

A fleck of spit landed on Miri's arm. Revolted, she quickly rubbed it off and took a tiny step sideways to avoid more. Carter, without noticing, did the same.

Get away from me, thought Miri. She sidled to the left again.

Again, Carter echoed her step.

Huh, thought Miri. Interesting. She took another tiny sideways step.

Carter followed, describing her short future in unpleasant detail.

Miri didn't dare look toward the shattered rim of the floorboards, but she could almost see it, hovering at the edge of her vision, a dark, empty crater on her left where the porch had been shelled. The important thing was to get close enough, but not too close. She took another tiny shuffle sideways.

Carter grinned, believing that she was shrinking with fear. Pleased to inspire terror, he pressed closer. "My sister had the misfortune to anger me, as you have . . ."

The dark hole yawned nearby; she could see it now. Just one more tiny step and they'd be in position. Miri stepped sideways.

Carter stepped sideways. ". . . a desperate fear of fire, I knew . . ."

Gazing deep into Carter's yellow eyes, Miri cleared her throat. "Swarm," she said.

For a split second, nothing happened. And then Miri heard a collective intake of breath, a shuffle, and a rush, and they were there—Ray, Robbie, and

Molly, dashing at Carter, weaving, jabbing, and pushing at him.

"What—stop, you—get away—" Carter, aggravated by the press of children, swatted at them wildly with his gun. "I'll get—hold still!"

"Ooooh, yah, Nick Car-tah!" squalled Ray.

"Yo, Nicky! The freaky monkey man!" hooted Robbie, darting forward to poke Carter in the neck.

"Stay back from the edge!" called Miri, as she bobbed up and down and stepped on Carter's foot.

Ray and Robbie began to kick at Carter's legs enthusiastically.

"Get away! What the devil?" Carter lifted a leg to kick back, got jabbed—this time by Robbie—lost his balance, and seesawed on the edge of the hole, flapping his arms. "You—" Carter's voice cracked with surprise as he felt the first pull of time's force.

The boys jogged toward him and back, poking with needling fingers, screeching like insane owls.

But they were too close! "Get back! Guys, get back!" called Miri, turning to push them to safety.

Carter saw his opportunity. His hand flashed out and seized her, a counterweight to the power pulling him in. At once, as his iron fingers curled around her arm, the fear that had stood to one side returned to

Miri in a rush. Her heart began to pound, her breath coming in gasps. Helplessly, she twisted in Carter's grasp. With a mighty shudder of panic, she tried to wrench her arm away and felt herself stumble, forward and down, toward the hole beneath the floor.

"*Miri!*" screamed Molly, and Ray and Robbie froze, paralyzed by the sight of their sister and their target locked together, swaying on the ruined edge of the floor.

"Gotcha!" roared Carter as he wavered, one hand holding his gun aloft, the other holding her tight. Miri was bent toward him, unable to resist the drag of time and man together.

An arm circled her waist, pulling her back.

But Carter, holding her wrist, was stronger.

She teetered, tried to balance, failed, and began the slow, irresistible fall forward. The arm around her middle tightened, strained, loosened, broke painfully open—

And there were just the two of them, Miri and Carter, falling together.

Then—

Ping. A bright gold coin—a ten-dollar eagle—spiraled up, twirling between her and Carter. For a split second, their eyes tracked it together, watching it rise, reach its apex, and begin to drop, sparkling, brilliant as fire—

Carter's hand shot up to grab the coin, releasing his hold on Miri's arm. As his fingers closed around the gold, Robbie grabbed Miri's freed hand and yanked with all his strength, pulling her back from the chasm. Turning, Miri caught a glimpse of Carter, saw his pale eyes open wide with the knowledge of what he'd just done, saw his mouth open in a silent O of shock—and then he tumbled, knocking back and forth like a rag in a hurricane as he dropped away into the darkness beneath the house.

Miri, saved, collapsed against Robbie, who collapsed in turn against Ray, who smacked into Molly, who dropped with a thud to the floor.

. . .

For a moment, they lay in a heap. Then, slowly, Robbie sat up. He leaned forward to gaze at the ragged rim of wood. "Et tu, Brute," he said solemnly.

There was a pause.

"What?" asked Ray.

"Julius Caesar," said Robbie.

There was another pause.

"Shut up," Ray said.

Miri lay in silence, staring at nothing. She was alive. She was safe. Her arm was throbbing where Carter had gripped it, but she was alive and safe. With an effort, she rolled over onto her stomach and reached for her sister's hand.

Molly's hand clutched hers tight. "Wow." She turned her head to the boys. "Good swarming."

Ray sat up. "I thought we were all goners."

"Me too," said Robbie. "I almost had a heart attack."

"The coin," murmured Miri. "Tossing the coin was brilliant."

"We knew how much he loved gold," Molly said, wiping her forehead with her sleeve.

"He loved it so much he *died*," said Robbie.

Miri and Molly looked at each other. "He's not dead," said Molly. "Not yet, anyway."

Robbie winced. "He's not coming back, is he?"

Miri shook her head. "He can't. I'm almost sure he can't."

"Good," said Ray.

Miri sat up, finally, and looked from brother to

sister to brother. "All of us did it. It was all of us that made it come out right. All of us together."

"It hasn't come out right yet," Ray pointed out. "There's still Mom."

"Compared to Carter, I'm not worried," Robbie said, smiling.

"Me neither," said Miri. In fact, she was longing to see their mother. "But let's do it together."

Ray and Robbie limped to their feet and gave their sisters a hand up. The four of them paused, facing the door, and then Robbie bowed to Miri. "After you."

Miri pushed it open. "Hey, Mom!" she bellowed. "We're home!"

. . .

Six days and one hundred and fifty years later, their mother stood in the doorway of the living room. "What are you doing?" she asked, eyeing her four older children, who were strewn, in angles ranging from fifty to hundred and eighty degrees, over the sofas and chairs.

"Math," mumbled Miri, her head bent over a tangle of numbers.

"Yeah," sighed Molly.

Her mother stared at Robbie. "Are you *reading*?" she asked.

"Yeah." A second passed and he looked up. "What?"

"Is it for school?"

He glanced at the spine. "Uh. No."

"It's for *fun*?" she pressed.

He nodded.

"What is it?" she asked, incredulous.

He looked at it again. "History book."

"A *history* book?"

He gave an exasperated sigh. "Yeah. A history book. Which I was, like, reading until you came in."

"Don't be sassy," she said, but absently. "A history book," she repeated. "About what?"

"Mom!" he yelled. "The Civil War! I'm trying to read!"

"The Civil War," she echoed in wonder. "You're reading a book about the Civil War." There was a pause. "We should ground you guys more often."

Silence.

"I mean, here you are, reading with your brother and sisters. Isn't it great? Isn't it cozy and nice?" She came in to peer over Robbie's shoulder. "History is *fascinating*, isn't it?"

Ray snorted. "Sometimes."

"And I'm so glad to see that you're taking an interest in the larger world," she went on enthusiastically. "Maybe it's because you've had some time and space for reflection, for *thinking*, you know?" She gave Robbie's shoulder a loving squeeze. "Being grounded is almost like a vacation in a way, isn't it?"

The four children lifted their heads and gave their mother four long, level stares.

"Well, fine," she said, taking a step backward. "But it was your own fault. It's a completely reasonable punishment, considering." She took another step backward. "Eleven thirty at night! Of all the ridiculous, impossible, irresponsible . . ." Her voice faded as she strode toward the kitchen.

Silence fell upon the living room again.

Some time later, Robbie lifted his eyes from his book. "It says here that no one ever saw him again. Carter, I mean. After the war, they don't know what happened to him."

"Good," said Ray. "I hope it hurt, whatever it was."

Again, silence.

Miri looked up. Cookie rounded the doorway and padded with businesslike efficiency to the sofa where Miri and Molly were curled. A quick leap put her in the middle of their legs, their papers, their pillows, and there she paced, carefully choosing the best available seat, which turned out to be atop Miri's open math book. She settled herself across the pages and waited expectantly.

"Hey, sweetie-Cookie," murmured Miri, glad for the interruption. For the past few days, Cookie had been disappearing for several hours at a stretch, returning to Miri and Molly with a distinctly well-fed and well-petted air. "You're going to get fat if you keep eating two centuries' worth of dinner," she whispered in the kitten's ear.

"What's that?" Molly said, leaning forward. "Around her neck?"

There was a small paper packet, attached in a yarn hammock around Cookie's neck. Miri held Cookie as Molly untied it and then unfolded the paper. Two delicate rings tumbled into her hand. She stared at them for a moment and then showed them to Miri. They were made of gold thread, braided together into a circlet, with a tiny flower tucked into the center.

Wordlessly, Molly handed Miri the paper they'd been wrapped in. *My dear little Gypsies, I don't know if these will reach you, but I think they may, and I hope you will accept them with my love. I have just received a ring myself, which I believe I must owe to some sort of enchantment cast by you girls and your darling kitten. My fiancé— you met him, I think—has named her Giddy, for the way she skitters out of his hands, but we are both very grateful to her and to you for introducing us. I have never been so happy! M*

Miri slipped the ring on her finger. It was light and pretty, just like Maudie. She looked up at Molly and saw that she had done the same. With their eyes, they shared the picture of Maudie, shining and joyful, her graceful fingers braiding the gold threads. She was in the house somewhere, in one of the layers of time suspended within its walls. And there, she was rapturously happy. They smiled at each other and, together, reached for Cookie and rubbed an ear apiece.

Cookie closed her eyes and purred.

AUTHOR'S NOTE

I was often hounded, as a child, by adults who wanted me to read educational books. Parents, librarians, and teachers—they all seemed to have some sort of obsession with making me learn while I was reading. "Here," they'd say, handing me a book with an awful title like *Nakyt of the Nile: A Girl's Life in Ancient Egypt,* "here is a wonderful book that will teach you all about pyramids!"

Bleah. Who cared about pyramids? All I wanted was a good story.

So it is with some embarrassment that I find that I have written a book that has history in it. I would be a good deal more embarrassed if it were a book *about* history, but it's not, I promise. It's *about* some kids who live in this very odd house and . . . well, you can read it yourself. But the story also includes some hunks of history, and though I have absolutely no intention of being educational, I have to confess: almost all of them are true.

If you are not interested in history, you can stop reading right now. But if you want to know more about the events and people mentioned in this book, here are the facts:

By the fall of 1864, the Civil War had been going on for three and a half years, and the United States— otherwise known as the Northerners, the Yankees, and the Union—was finally winning. In Virginia, the Confederates—otherwise known as the Rebels, the Southerners—had been pushed down into the southern part of the state, leaving the northern part under Union control. But Union control was not very controlled, due to the activities of Colonel John Singleton Mosby (the Colonel of our story), who had been given command of a cavalry battalion in 1863 for the express purpose of "annoying" the Union army in northern Virginia. Mosby was an expert annoyer, and by the fall of 1864, when our story intersects his, he and his band of several hundred Rangers had enjoyed fifteen months of sneaking around, shooting up stray Yankee soldiers, robbing trains, and kidnapping Union officers for the fun of it.

In August of '64, the commander of the Union forces, General Ulysses S. Grant, ordered Major General Phil Sheridan and his army to rid the Shenandoah Valley, a long river valley that runs along the western border of the state of Virginia, of all Confederate troops, and, for emphasis, to burn crops as he went. Sheridan gladly obeyed. "The people must be left with nothing," he wrote, "but their eyes to weep with." By mid-October, Sheridan was triumphant: the Confederate army had been pushed south, and the finest farmland in the Confederacy was a scorched wasteland, leaving the locals hard-pressed to feed themselves, much less the Rebel army.

It was at this point that the Battle of Cedar Creek, gleefully reenacted by Ray, Robbie, and Ollie the Rot King, occurred. A cranky old Confederate general named Jubal Early (really!) decided to stage a surprise attack on Sheridan's troops at a spot called Cedar Creek. In the middle of the night of October 18–19, while Sheridan was absent in Washington, twenty thousand Confederate troops snuck into position around the sleeping Yankees at Cedar

Creek and struck at dawn. The Union soldiers, waking to find themselves under attack, ran like rabbits. At the same time, about fifteen miles to the north, Sheridan was making his way back to camp, enjoying an early morning ride, when he heard the sounds of gunfire. Perplexed, he urged his horse to a trot—and then a gallop—toward Cedar Creek, and was greeted by the sight of his own army streaming toward him in full retreat.

Upon seeing their commander, the defeated soldiers began to cheer, and this threw Sheridan into a monumental rage. "God damn you, don't you cheer me! If you love your country, come up to the front!" he screamed, in addition to a whole lot of others things that can't be put in a book for kids, all the while tearing toward what was left of his camp. Inspired by his courage—and also probably afraid of what he'd do to them if they continued to retreat—his men turned around and followed him back to the front lines, where they fought again and succeeded in turning a humiliating defeat into a major Union victory.

Mosby did not take part in that battle, but he was fully aware of Sheridan's other activities. Throughout August, September, and October, as Sheridan rampaged through the Valley, Mosby's attacks on Union soldiers, trains, and supplies were frequent, violent, and successful. In mid-August, several weeks into his Valley Campaign and angry that his hard fighting hadn't produced more control over the conquered territory, Sheridan decided to take action. He assigned a special unit, called the Scouts, to the task of "cleaning out Mosby's gang."

What followed was a month of raids, gunfights, attacks, and counterattacks. Usually, the Union got the worst of it. Mosby was a brilliant strategist, his men were outstanding fighters, and all of them knew the territory far better than their opponents.

But it was during one such attack that the Rangers made a fatal error: they shot a Union soldier as he was surrendering. Though this might seem like a minor consideration in the middle of a war, when the whole point is to kill the enemy, it was, on the contrary, seen as a shocking breach of the rules of combat: a soldier who surrendered was to be made prisoner, not killed.

When Sheridan's officers heard of this, they decided on their revenge: they would treat any captured Ranger as a criminal, rather than as a soldier. This meant that the Northerners would execute any Ranger, any suspected Ranger, or anyone helping a Ranger immediately and without investigation. No questions, no trials, and no prisoners.

On September 23, 1864, in the small town of Front Royal, they put their new policy into action, taking six captured Rangers out of the makeshift jail where they were held and swiftly executing them, four by firing squad and two by hanging. One of the victims was a seventeen-year-old boy who was not a member of the Rangers at all.

Mosby in his turn was outraged and swore vengeance. As he wrote to General Robert E. Lee in late October, "It is my purpose to hang an equal number of Custer's men whenever I capture them," a plan he made good on November 6, when five Union soldiers were hanged by a group of Rangers.

It is into this context—the late-October collection of Union soldiers for Mosby's revenge killings—that I dropped Robbie and Ray and let them fall into the hands of Nick Carter.

I regret to report that Nick Carter was a real person and evidently just as foul as I have portrayed him here. His true name was Loughborough Carter, but everyone called him Nick, a name his father bestowed upon him because he behaved like Old Nick; that is, the devil. According to John Munson, a

Ranger who wrote a memoir of his service entitled *Reminiscences of a Mosby Guerilla,* Nick Carter and his pal Charley McDonough were "outlaws who accompanied us only by the tolerance of the Colonel. . . . Nick Carter belonged to one of the oldest and most aristocratic families in Virginia, but he accumulated such a load of undesirable responsibility and notoriety during the war that he thought it best to leave the country mysteriously at its close." Though Carter cannot be definitely traced after the war, local legend has it that he went to Mexico, where he made a living shooting bandits.

As for the other Rangers that make an appearance in *Magic in the Mix*, there was an "uncouth" Ranger named John Hearn, who served as the pattern for the Hern of our story. He was said to look "every inch a clumsy clown in a sea of trouble." Charlie, on the other hand, is a fictional creation, inspired by a photograph of a Ranger with an enormous black moustache. The gunfight that occurs in Miri and Molly's front yard is, likewise, fictional, but it is based on the descriptions of several typical Ranger engagements in 1864.

I admit to a sneaking fondness for Colonel John Singleton Mosby, despite his poor taste in choosing sides in the Civil War. I like him partly because he was so brilliant at what he did, and partly because he seemed to have such a good time doing it. I'm not alone in my partiality; even his enemies admired him. At the end of the war, when there was a price on Mosby's head as a fugitive criminal, Ulysses Grant himself intervened to save his life. Mosby, in return, became a supporter of Grant in the 1870s when he ran for president.

One final historical note: it may seem unlikely to twenty-first-century readers that anyone would take thirteen-year-old boys seriously as a soldiers, but teenage soldiers were common on both sides during the Civil War. The youngest registered Ranger in Mosby's 43rd was only fourteen years old, and boys as young as twelve served as drummer boys in both armies. In addition, despite all the current hand-wringing about our diets, they are a major improvement over the Civil War era in terms of vitamins, minerals, and protein. And, accordingly, height and weight. Colonel Mosby, who was about 5'7" and weighed 128 pounds, would be unlikely to consider the average-size Ray and Robbie too small to be soldiers.

ACKNOWLEDGMENTS

A work of fiction that contains historical fact requires considerably more gratitude than one that's entirely made up. In researching the Civil War action in the Shenandoah Valley in general, and Mosby's 43rd Virginia Cavalry Battalion in particular, I have relied upon *Mosby's Rangers*, by Jeffry Wert; *Reminisences of a Mosby Guerrilla*, by John W. Munson; and *The Memoirs of Colonel John S. Mosby*, by Mosby himself. For Civil War–era expressions and slang, my source has been *The Language of the Civil War*, by John D. Wright. I have appreciated the maps and descriptions of various battles published by the Civil War Trust at www.civilwar.org/ and the meticulous Order of Battle for the Battle of Cedar Creek, published by

the National Park Service at www.nps.gov/cebe
/historyculture/order-of-battle-battle-of-cedar
-creek.htm

I am profoundly grateful to the librarians and researchers at the Ruth E. Lloyd Information Center (RELIC) for genealogy and local history at the Bull Run Regional Library of the Prince William Public Library System, where Tish Como, Beverly Veness, and Margaret Binning managed to track down in a matter of days a trove of information about Nick Carter that had eluded me for months. I salute their research skills. Further thanks are due to Joe Molinaro, who assisted me with matters pertaining to Civil War geography; to my sister, Sally Barrows, who helped with regional information; and to my daughter Esme, who provided authoritative linguistic advice about thirteen-year-olds.

As always, I am relieved and grateful to be able to conduct my primary research at the University Library at the University of California, Berkeley. Without the resources I find there, most of my books would never have seen the light of day.